'You came bac[k]

He spoke, the dee[p]
fitting the massive [
lights disappeared. [
in trouble.'

'Why did you come back?'

'Because I wouldn't have left a dog, let alone another human being, in trouble on a night like this. There's no need to take it so personally.'

There had been no need for him to be so rude, Jessica thought wrathfully.

Dear Reader

In Australia, Marion Lennox has Nikki and Luke find a STORM HAVEN; Laura MacDonald's Toni finds herself IN AT THE DEEP END with her new boss in Africa; at the health centre, Margaret O'Neill's Dr Ben Masters becomes NO LONGER A STRANGER to Clare Lucas; and we meet Michael Knight again—first seen in PRIDE'S FALL—in Flora Sinclair's KNIGHT'S MOVE as he meets his match in Jessica Balfour. Happy New Year!

The Editor

Flora Sinclair was born in and grew up outside London. She went north to study psychology at university, but returned to work in a London hospital. She now lives in Scotland, dividing her time between Glasgow and a remote Hebridean island.

Recent titles by the same author:

PRIDE'S FALL
DOCTOR ALONE

KNIGHT'S MOVE

BY
FLORA SINCLAIR

MILLS & BOON

MILLS & BOON LIMITED
ETON HOUSE, 18–24 PARADISE ROAD
RICHMOND, SURREY, TW9 1SR

DID YOU PURCHASE THIS BOOK WITHOUT A COVER?

If you did, you should be aware it is **stolen property** as it was reported *unsold and destroyed* by a retailer. Neither the Author nor the publisher has received any payment for this book.

All the characters in this book have no existence outside the imagination of the Author, and have no relation whatsoever to anyone bearing the same name or names. They are not even distantly inspired by any individual known or unknown to the Author, and all the incidents are pure invention.

All Rights Reserved. The text of this publication or any part thereof may not be reproduced or transmitted in any form or by any means, electronic or mechanical, including photocopying, recording, storage in an information retrieval system, or otherwise, without the written permission of the publisher.

This book is sold subject to the condition that it shall not, by way of trade or otherwise, be lent, resold, hired out or otherwise circulated without the prior consent of the publisher in any form of binding or cover other than that in which it is published and without a similar condition including this condition being imposed on the subsequent purchaser.

MILLS & BOON, the Rose Device and LOVE ON CALL are trademarks of the publisher.

First published in Great Britain 1995 by Mills & Boon Limited

© Flora Sinclair 1995

Australian copyright 1995   Philippine copyright 1995 This edition 1995

ISBN 0 263 78918 7

Set in 10 on 12 pt Linotron Times 03-9501-54687

Typeset in Great Britain by Centracet, Cambridge Made and printed in Great Britain

CHAPTER ONE

THE tail-lights of the car shone ahead of her in the distance with a comforting red glow in the otherwise blackness of the winter night. Jessica concentrated on her driving—telling herself she should never have been on the road didn't help matters one bit and only served to underline the gravity of her situation. The whole day was a series of 'if onlys'... If only she hadn't overslept; if only there hadn't been a problem with the car; if only... The biggest 'if only' intruded. If only her aunt hadn't been ill she wouldn't have had to make this journey at all, just when the winter weather was so bad. If only she had come up to see her aunt in the summer when she had promised. If only... But there was no point in going on. And on. She *was* on the road. The blizzard *was* getting worse. Her only option was to keep going.

Her headlamps were penetrating less and less into the darkness and, where they did pierce it, all they illustrated was swirling whiteness. Jessica fixed her eyes firmly on the lights of the car in front. That at least confirmed she wasn't totally alone in this white wasteland and kept a damper on her wilder fantasies. It was all too easy to see ghostly shapes appearing out of the dark through the swirling snow. And surely there couldn't be a part of the Scottish Highlands that *didn't* lend itself to, at the very least, the possibility of haunting. There was a village not much further where she could take shelter, she fervently hoped and prayed.

But without the reassuring presence of the car in front she wasn't sure that she would make it. It was a talisman, assuring her she hadn't got lost somewhere on the hills.

Was it her imagination or did the lights in front seem to be getting further away? The twists and curves in the road meant they were often lost to sight for a few bleak moments, but they always reappeared. Now the red lights seemed to be—no, they were—getting smaller. It wasn't an illusion caused by the worsening snow conditions. If she lost sight of them. . . Panic flared momentarily within her and without thinking she pressed her foot down hard on the accelerator. The little car shot forward and from then on Jessica was never sure what happened. All she knew was that the skid had landed her in the ditch at the side of the road, with the front half of the car buried in a snow bank. A sickening thud indicated there was something solid under the snow—a fact which seemed to be confirmed as the engine screeched, then died with the impact. The lights went out and she was plunged into utter darkness.

Without conscious thought Jessica looked in the direction of the other car, her eyes scouring the winter blackness for a reassuring red light. But it was too far ahead now and she could see nothing. Stifling a scream before it could fully form in her throat, she valiantly strove to control a rising panic, groping on the seat beside her for her flashlight. With the familiar golden glow brightening the interior of the car she felt instantly better.

As she opened the car door with the intention of checking the damage the swirling snow and frigid temperature convinced her it wasn't worth it. There was absolutely nothing she could do even if she did survey the damage, since her knowledge of cars and their workings was only slightly greater than her understanding of the second law of thermodynamics. Slamming the door quickly to conserve the fast dissipating heat in the car, Jessica was glad she had had the foresight to come prepared for an emergency. Her friends often laughed at her tendency to prepare for any eventuality, but she well knew that in the Scottish Highlands in winter any eventuality was always a distinct possibility.

She had a hot drink, some food and, most important of all, a sleeping-bag in the body of the car with her. While she might be uncomfortable, she wouldn't die of hypothermia. Leaving the car would be the worst thing she could do. Her major problem overnight would be if the snow continued and drifted—she might get buried. That was another thought she pushed out of her mind, along with visions of long-dead clansmen coming down the hills to see what had disturbed their centuries of peace. Concentrating on the practical, she knew the first thing to do was get in the sleeping-bag before she lost any more body heat. As she twisted round to pull it from the back seat she was amazed to see lights coming towards her.

Another car was on the road! Something struck her as odd about the lights, but all she could think of was that she wasn't alone and someone was about to prove themselves her saviour. Surely no one would refuse to give her a lift, given the circumstances. It was then that she realised what was troubling her. There were white and *red* lights coming towards her. As she was working out what was happening the body of the car reversing towards her split the snow. Barely had she registered that it had stopped before icy air was blasting around her as the door was wrenched open and a deep male voice, heavy with sarcasm, echoed out of the darkness.

'A woman! I might have known!'

A strong hand fastened itself around her wrist and pulled her out of the car, almost dragging her across the icy road before pushing her into the blessedly warm interior of another car. He followed almost immediately through the driver's door and Jessica was only dimly aware of him throwing her overnight bag on to the back seat.

'What are you doing?' It might not have been the most sensible question in the world, but it was all Jessica could think of at the time. She wasn't prepared, however, for the look of contempt the man gave her.

'Rescuing you!' he answered harshly. 'Now, shut up and let me concentrate on getting us out of here!'

For a minute Jessica was only too pleased to do that and leave her immediate future in the capable hands of this giant of a man, who could make even the interior of a Range Rover seem crowded. There was an agonising moment when the wheels only spun on the icy road surface, but then they caught and the car slowly moved forward and Jessica let out a breath she hadn't realised she had been holding. She thought the man next to her twitched at the sound, but nothing was said by either of them.

As the shock subsided, Jessica began to take an active interest in her rescuer. At the moment all she could see was a massive if well-shaped pair of hands on the steering-wheel. Risking a sidelong glance at him, she discovered that the collar of his sheepskin jacket was still turned up, shielding most of his face from her. All she could distinguish for the moment was a thatch of deep golden-blond hair, which flopped forward across his forehead, and a decidedly determined nose.

'Where are we going?' It was worth risking a snub, she felt, to find out what his plans were for her.

'*We*,' he replied, with heavy emphasis on the single syllable, 'are making for the first sign of habitation.'

'You came back for me.' It wasn't a question yet lacked the certainty of a statement. She waited for a moment, but there was no response. 'How did you know?'

Just when she thought he was going to ignore the direct question he spoke, the deep resonance of his voice fitting the massive body it came from.

'Your lights disappeared. There wasn't anywhere you could have gone legitimately. You obviously had to be in trouble. I'd already noticed you had been driving more and more slowly.'

'You mean, you were waiting for me?'

No reply.

'Why did you come back?'

Silence.

'Why?'

The peremptory tone maybe hadn't been the best one to have used—she noticed the giant's shoulders stiffen and she had the sense that he would have turned away from her if the car had given him anywhere to go. 'Please tell me. I. . .' She was horrified to hear her voice falter as the shock of her accident and her luck in being rescued coalesced into an overwhelming weariness and the desire to have a good cry.

This time something in her voice must have reached him because he relaxed slightly and answered her, even if the response he gave wasn't the most friendly in the world.

'Because I wouldn't have left a dog, let alone another human being, in trouble on a night like this. There's no need to take it so personally.'

Feeling thoroughly snubbed and put in her place, Jessica turned from the man to gaze through the windscreen at the swirling snowflakes caught in the yellow beam of the headlights in front of her. Even as she watched the snow got thicker. The flush that had burned her cheeks at the man's words faded. There had been no need for him to be so rude, she thought wrathfully. But, whatever his failings as far as manners went, he *had* come back for her!

'It might not be personal to *you*, but it is to *me*. It was, after all, me whom you rescued! I want to thank you for that.'

Again silence greeted her remark and Jessica's temper began its slow burn. He might have rescued her from a very nasty predicament but that didn't, in her opinion, excuse his current lack of manners. For someone who had put himself out for her he seemed to be displaying remarkably little grace in the situation. After all, she reasoned, she hadn't asked to be rescued, had she? She would have been perfectly all right in the car—she had had her emergency supplies.

A little voice told her that she might very well *not* have been all right and that she should just be thankful he had come back for her and not expect anything else of him. With the weather continuing to worsen the road might well have become impassable, and if another car hadn't come along she would have been in very deep trouble. Nevertheless, there was something about this man's manner that made her want to assert herself, show some spark of independence and self-reliance. Thoughtlessly she rushed into speech.

'It was, of course, extremely kind of you, but not wholly necessary. I would have been perfectly all right until morning.'

'Don't be stupid. You would have frozen to death!'

'I had a sleeping-bag!'

A disgusted grunt and muttered exclamation which she didn't quite catch told her what he thought of her sleeping-bag. Knowing she should keep quiet, nevertheless, something prompted Jessica into further speech—even though she knew that by now she was being at least as rude as he was.

'I suppose the story will be good for your macho image. A knight riding to the rescue of some poor, incompetent damsel—even if you have got a Range Rover rather than a white charger!'

To her surprise, she thought she detected a very slight thawing in his manner and she had the distinct impression that something she had said amused him. This seemed to be borne out by his response to this piece of ungraciousness.

'As you say, anything to maintain my knightly image.'

Stung, Jessica retorted, 'And do you make a habit of rescuing damsels in distress?'

His wry, 'It has been known,' was not what Jessica had expected and hinted at things about which she knew nothing.

Since there seemed to be nothing to add to this comment—which Jessica thought somewhat self-satisfied—for once she wisely remained silent.

Their speed was little more than a crawl, the windscreen-wipers struggling to keep up with the demands being made on them, when lights finally shone out of the night at them. Jessica was so mesmerised by the swirling snow that she almost missed them.

'Lights ahead!' she exclaimed, and was put out by the calm response of the man at her side.

'I've already seen them.'

He seemed to know where he was going because they passed a couple of houses and slid to a stop in front of a small hotel. Without looking at her, the man issued curt instructions.

'Wait here. I'll go and investigate.'

He was out of the car before Jessica had time to reply and she was left grinding her teeth in annoyance. He might be the modern equivalent of a knight in shining armour, but he was also a very irritating man. It crossed Jessica's mind that maybe medieval maidens had also found chivalrous knights smug and irritating. It was a peculiarly comforting thought. Lost in daydreams of knights in armour fighting fire-breathing dragons, she was unprepared for his climbing back into the car and reaching into the back not only for her overnight case, but his also.

'Come on. Don't just sit there.' He was out of the door again and striding through the blizzard while Jessica was still unbuckling her seatbelt.

As she slipped and slid her way to the welcoming lights, a myriad thoughts flashed through Jessica's overactive mind. Romantic and not so romantic stories of strangers sharing rooms were uppermost as she pushed her way into the over furnished entrance lobby where a tiny, plump middle-aged woman bustled forward, exclaiming at the sight of her.

'Och, you poor wee soul! To be out in such weather! Come away into the fire and let your husband sort things out.'

Jessica shot her companion a look of pure outrage but it was lost on the broad, sheepskin-clad back, and without a word she allowed herself to be led away.

In a matter of moments she was seated by a blazing log fire, a tray of tea in front of her and a large glass of whisky in her hand. There was nothing, according to Mrs Gordon—for so she had introduced herself—like a drop of the hard stuff for warding off a chill and putting the world to rights. Promising them some hot soup in a moment, that lady hurried away, leaving Jessica alone.

But not for long. A noise at the door attracted her attention and she turned to glare at the man who was her rescuer as he came in. It was the first good look she had got of him and, despite herself, she was impressed. His head seemed to brush the top of the doorway as he walked through and she guessed him to be in his mid-thirties. The determined nose, already glimpsed, was matched by an equally forthright jaw. To add to this, set in a lean face, above high, chiselled cheekbones, were the bluest eyes she could remember seeing. Eyes which were gazing at her unflinchingly. It was a gaze which was difficult to hold and her embarrassed attention settled on his remarkable eyebrows. Of obviously different shapes, one being smoothly arched and the other much flatter, they gave him a look of cynical enquiry which added to, rather than detracted from his attraction. The blond hair shone silver in the lamplight and he exuded an air of masculine strength—a power—emphasised by the breadth of his shoulders which, Jessica could see, owed nothing to the padding of the sheepskin.

'I've taken the bags up,' he informed her, folding long legs in immaculately cut fine wool trousers—now showing signs of damp around their bottoms—into the chair opposite her. Jessica, who had been aware of cutting a very dowdy figure in comparison with her stunning companion, had her attention once more brought back to the unconventionality of her situation.

'Have you indeed?' she all but snapped at him, conscious of the man's attraction but determined to make it clear to him that, confusion over status or not, availability of rooms or not, she wasn't sharing a room with him. If it came to it, she could bed down in front of the fire for the night.

'Is something the matter?' He was pouring tea for himself since Jessica had neglected to do it for him, although he didn't seem bothered or surprised by the omission. His very imperturbability pushed Jessica into speaking rashly.

'Why did you let them think we are married? I'm not sharing a room with you.'

Navy blue eyes turned icy and pierced into her. 'You should wait until you're asked,' he shot back harshly. 'It was a natural mistake. One, I might add, you did nothing to correct.'

Did he give her an odd glance at that? Jessica wondered, but decided it was her imagination.

'A mistake I've now corrected, and have explained the full circumstances. Your virtue——' an ironically quirked brow implied 'such as it is' '—is quite safe. For tonight, at least.'

Feeling silly and gauche, and knowing that she wasn't behaving like herself, Jessica murmured, 'Sorry,' under her breath.

As though she hadn't responded, he went on, 'Mr Gordon would like you to register some time. I didn't know your name.'

'Yes, of course.' Feeling even more like an adolescent schoolgirl, Jessica struggled to raise her head and look at this very aloof stranger, wondering what he thought of her. She needn't have worried; his attention was firmly fixed on his tea and a totally uninterested expression on his face told its own story. His complete lack of awareness gave Jessica the impetus to get control of herself and, with a mental shake, she decided that they should at least put their very irregular relationship on a more formal footing. Taking a steadying breath, she faced him, suggesting, 'Maybe we should introduce ourselves. I'm Jessica Balfour.' She held out her hand and surprised a sudden flash in the blue eyes.

'Knight,' he announced, taking her hand in his own large one. Which left Jessica floundering, as that was all he appeared to be going to say. Night? What was he talking about? It was an odd greeting—or did he intend it to mean goodnight? She remembered her comments in the car. Was he referring to himself as her knight in shining armour? As she realised that she must still be in some kind of shock, the penny finally dropped. Just about the same time that he decided to help her out.

'Michael Knight.'

Jessica looked at him, stunned by the coincidence of his name, her skin heating to a delicate pink as she once more recalled the remarks she had made about knights rescuing damsels in distress. She felt all kinds of fool, and only the knowledge that he would know she couldn't possibly have known his name made the situation bearable.

Trying to hide her embarrassment and momentary lapse, Jessica plunged on. 'I would like to thank you again, Mr Knight, for your help tonight. I'm——'

But it seemed she was destined not to tell him how very grateful she was as Mrs Gordon chose that moment to come in with a tray laden with bowls of steaming soup.

'I hope this is all right, Doctor, and you don't mind eating in here. We're not really open for guests at the moment and the dining-room isn't very warm. You'll be more comfortable here.'

So he was a doctor. Jessica wondered why he hadn't corrected her earlier and looked at him anew, this time more closely, wondering where he worked and what kind of doctor he was. Dr Knight, however, was already on his feet, taking the laden tray from Mrs Gordon to place it on the low table.

'We'll do very well, thank you, Mrs Gordon. It's good of you to go to the trouble.' Jessica could barely believe her eyes as he gave the older woman a smile of such warmth and charm that she positively glowed under it. 'And may I introduce Miss Balfour?'

Jessica smiled to herself, but said nothing. Two could play the deception game. If he hadn't seen fit to correct her misconception she didn't see why she should correct his. There was time enough to correct him. So she let the introduction stand.

Jessica hadn't thought she was hungry but the savoury smell of the soup tempted her to try it, and before she knew what she had been doing the bowl was empty in front of her. In her haste to be on her way and make up lost time she had skipped lunch, making do with a chocolate bar in the car. Her stomach was reminding her of this, sending appreciative messages as a wonderfully fragrant meat pie was put before them.

Some time ago Jessica had given up eating red meat as part of a healthy eating plan, but even as her mind was telling her it would be unforgivably rude to reject Mrs Gordon's hospitality her stomach was signalling, Don't you dare! Her companion apparently had no such dietary scruples and was, Jessica realised, looking at her with ill-concealed impatience, waiting for her to start so that he could begin his own meal.

Giving him a shaky smile, Jessica picked up her knife and fork, feeling slightly contrite. Keeping that vast frame fuelled must take some fairly hefty meals.

It wasn't that there was anything fat or soft about him, just a broad frame of solid muscle which stretched up to what Jessica guessed to be a towering six feet five. Remembering his grip on her wrist as he'd hauled her out of the car, Jessica acknowledged that his strength obviously matched his size. She was hardly petite herself.

All in all she would not have expected him to be a doctor. At the very least he should have been some sort of explorer—something very outdoor, rugged and macho. He would look at home in the wild open spaces of nature at her most elemental. She reviewed his behaviour. The macho bit was there all right. Yet as she sat opposite him, with the deep red glow from the fire casting interesting shadows across his face, there was something calming, almost soothing about him and his profession seemed more feasible after all. And his size would have made a very welcome addition to the rugby team when he was a medical student. Probably for a while after that, too.

As the edge of her appetite dulled Jessica realised that neither of them had spoken. With that realisation, what had been companionable silence now seemed awkward and self-conscious. Or was it only she who experienced the silence as such? Telling herself it was only good manners rather than active curiosity which was prompting her to speech, Jessica opened her mouth to ask Dr Knight where he had come from and where he was going.

Almost as though he had been waiting for her, Dr Knight chose that moment to speak and throughout the rest of the meal and the coffee directed the conversation into purely impersonal channels. As soon as he decently could, once the meal was over, he made his excuses and left. Jessica watched him go, frustrated on two counts—firstly that she hadn't found anything out about her rescuer at all, and secondly that she clearly didn't hold out enough interest to detain this very attractive man for a second longer than was polite.

He had gone by the time she was up the next morning, and Jessica felt unaccountably cheated—even when she discovered that he had arranged for her car to be collected, and for her to hire a car if she needed to. It told her so clearly that he had meant what he had said—he was only doing what he would for anyone. There was nothing personal in it.

Jessica caught sight of herself in the mirror by Reception. Without conceit she knew that she was more than averagely attractive. Her dark hair curled softly round a heart-shaped face whose high cheekbones set off her large, dark brown eyes. If she thought her mouth a trifle too large other people didn't. She was used to turning heads and frowned as she realised that this time, for some reason, her looks had failed to please. She shrugged. It didn't really matter. He was only some passing stranger and she wasn't so insecure that she had to conquer every man she met, was she? She shrugged again. He definitely didn't matter. But at the back of her mind a voice was protesting.

CHAPTER TWO

'I'VE had a good idea.'

Jessica's claim was greeted by a concerted chorus of moans, groans and disbelief.

'I don't want to hear it.' Naomi Reid spoke more forcefully than usual, as though by the very power of her words she could blot out those Jessica had just uttered.

'Never again. You promised. Never again.' Stuart James shook his head.

Two student nurses unobtrusively headed for the door.

'What's the matter?' Jessica was completely confused. 'All I said was——'

'We know what you said,' Naomi interrupted repressively. 'What we don't, we really don't want to hear is what follows.'

'Why?' Jessica was all injured innocence. 'I just thought——'

The phone went and Naomi and Stuart both lunged towards it; the student nurses vanished out of the door and Jessica realised she had lost her audience. It *was* a good idea—she just knew it was. Stuart was still on the phone and Naomi had put the kettle on, the simple task of making coffee taking much more of her attention than it did normally, when the door opened again and Dr Val Forrester lumbered in, panting slightly, and headed straight for the large armchair before collapsing into it. At forty-one she was expecting her first, much longed-for child, and at only just over five months looked as though she was about to give birth to twins, at the very least. As the other occupants of the room regarded her with various degrees of concern in their eyes she struggled to sit upright. Everyone worried about her, since the pregnancy hadn't been completely easy, but no one wanted to worry her more by showing their concern and she firmly resisted coddling. Now she fixed them with her clear grey eyes.

'Why are you looking at me like that? What's wrong?' She sounded slightly defensive and Naomi rushed into speech.

'I hope you're both feeling strong. I would hate to shock you into a premature labour.' She laughed as she said the words, taking any sting out of them, and Val nodded her acceptance of the concern and care that lay behind them.

'Well?'

Naomi and Stuart looked at each other, then slowly turned to focus their regard on Jessica.

'Tell Val what you told us,' Stuart instructed in his most authoritarian voice.

'I didn't get a chance to tell you anything,' Jessica complained with what she felt was righteous indignation.

'You told us the most important—the worst part,' Naomi pointed out tartly and Jessica affected an expression of deep hurt.

'Will someone tell me what is going on?' Val Forrester demanded and two of her staff looked at the third, raising their eyebrows in identical expressions of disdain.

'Tell her,' Stuart commanded.

Jessica sighed deeply—never was anyone so misunderstood. 'All I got as far as saying,' she explained to her boss, 'was that I'd had a good idea.'

Before she could get any further her words were cut short by the shout of laughter from the older woman, then the other two cracked up and Jessica was left totally bewildered by her three colleagues, who seemed totally unable to control their mirth.

Her, 'I don't see what's so funny,' only brought forth further gales of laughter.

Val wiped tears from her eyes and clutched at her sides. 'Stop it. Don't make me laugh any more—it *will* send me into labour.'

As the other members of the day hospital team drifted into the staffroom for their beginning-of-the-week meeting the laughter gradually subsided, but as the news that Jessica had had 'a good idea' spread round them shouts of laughter—or expressions of horror, depending on who heard the news—made themselves evident.

The business of the meeting concluded, Val turned to her senior registrar. 'Well, I suppose we'd better hear it before the suspense kills one of us.'

Now it was Jessica's turn to pretend to be huffy. 'After the way you've all been treating me I'm not sure that I do want to tell you,' she informed them loftily. 'All I said was——'

'No, not again,' Val interrupted hastily. 'I don't think we could stand that expression again.'

'What's so funny?' Jessica asked, apparently genuinely ignorant as to why a seemingly innocent expression should have caused such mayhem.

Naomi took pity on her and explained. 'It's how you introduced your last "idea"—you know, the small research project that now takes up every spare second we have, not to mention the space to store all the assessment forms, and turns our dreams into nightmares when we contemplate having to code the data, then analyse it and——'

'OK so it's a bit bigger than we thought,' Jessica admitted with a shrug, 'but you have to agree that we're getting heaps out of it——'

'Oh, *heaps*,' Stuart agreed ironically.

'The new idea?' Val reminded Jessica, butting in to keep the peace.

'Well,' Jessica began, taking a deep breath as she prepared herself to launch what she just knew was a great idea. 'Well, I thought we ought to organise an art exhibition.'

The silence that greeted her statement was underwhelming.

'Is that it?' Stuart asked almost disbelievingly. 'An art exhibition?' As the team's registrar, he was clearly less than impressed.

'Is that all?' Sally, one of the student nurses, sounded thoroughly disappointed and even Val looked let down.

Jessica stared at them. How could they be so blind? So apathetic? Couldn't they see the possibilities? Her dark eyes glowed with the fire of enthusiasm.

'No. Don't you see?' Jessica began to elaborate, the excitement in her voice forcing the others to pay her more attention. 'I mean a proper exhibition, next summer, with artwork from all over Scotland—and not just from patients but from relatives and staff too. And all on the theme of mental illness. What it means to people, how it affects them, how it has changed their lives. Relatives and staff have as much to say about that as patients do. They may not be the first-hand voices of illness but the impact on their—on our lives is important, too. We can use this to try to explain to the public what mental illness is about—use it as a way to educate them. Try to make them feel less threatened, less afraid. Get them to understand it a bit more.'

'It's possible.' Graham, the staff nurse, looked brighter and grinned at Jessica. He was obviously beginning to see the same possibilities she did.

'Maybe.' Stuart was still sceptical.

'Where were you thinking of having this?' Val asked, frowning as she mentally flicked through possibilities. 'One of the galleries in town?'

'No, no. Here.' Jessica sounded almost impatient as her friends and colleagues struggled to keep up with her ideas. 'Don't you see? It's an ideal way of getting people into the day hospital, so that they can have a look round and see how ordinary it all is. You know how most people don't like hospitals, and psychiatric facilities in particular. They'll come here—'

She was cut off as Val held up her hand. 'I can see you've been putting a lot of thought into this,' she told the younger woman with a smile, 'but we haven't got time to discuss it now. Why don't we all have a think about it and discuss it properly at a meeting later in the week? What about first thing Wednesday? By then we'll have had a chance to think about it and ask the patients for their views, and you can give us a better idea of what you're planning.'

Jessica wasn't totally happy at being put off, but knew better than to argue. At least having a couple of days would give her a chance to work on some of them. Graham was the obvious place to start since he had already expressed an interest. The fact that maybe this stemmed from the crush he had on her as much as her 'good idea' she refused to consider. She would simply make the most of his enthusiasm and support.

Shona Whyte waddled into Jessica's room, the broad grin on her chubby face alerting Jessica to the fact that something out of the ordinary had happened.

'Great idea, the exhibition.' Shona collapsed into the chair Jessica held steady for her, grinning up at her doctor. 'I'll get Barry to put in some photos.'

'Who told you?' Jessica was amazed that anyone outside the immediate day-hospital patients knew.

Shona's airy, 'Oh, everyone's talking about it,' threw her.

'I didn't know Barry was a photographer.' Barry was Shona's husband and Shona nodded vigorously and launched into a song of praise over his talents.

Jessica watched and listened carefully for any sign that Shona's exuberance was shading over into mania but could find none. So far, so good.

She remembered the day nearly six months ago when Shona had told her the exciting and worrying news.

'I'm pregnant!' The woman had blurted the words out, her eyes fixed on Jessica's face, and then promptly burst into tears.

Leaping from her chair, Jessica had put her arms round her patient and rocked her gently. 'Why the tears? I thought you wanted a baby? You *both* wanted a baby.' Her heart had turned over as she'd rapidly reviewed her patient's medication.

'We do,' the woman sobbed, struggling to get control of her tears.

'Well, then?'

'Now I'm pregnant, I'm scared. I——'

'We'll sort it out. You'll be fine,' Jessica interrupted. 'Just how pregnant are you?'

'About six weeks.'

'We'll need to review your medication.'

Shona turned anguished eyes back to Jessica. 'That's what I thought. And that's what worries me. You know my history. You know how bad I am when I'm manic. I'm really worried that being pregnant might start it up again. Much as I want this baby, I don't think I could go through that again. And what if I get post-natal depression? Suppose I can't look after the baby? Suppose I do something to the baby? Suppose—'

'Whoa! Hold it right there. You're rushing ahead of yourself. We've got seven and a half months to work on you *not* getting manic or depressed. After you and your husband wanting a baby for so long, nothing is going to stop you enjoying this one!'

'Are you sure?'

'Positive!' Jessica mentally crossed her fingers. She was by no means certain, but didn't think it would do Mrs Whyte's mental condition any good to say so just at the moment.

Shona Whyte was taking both lithium and nardil for her bipolar illness. The lithium would have to stay, but she would need to come off the nardil. It was a pity that she had got pregnant while taking it. Shona would need a lot of support to get her through this pregnancy, but Jessica had no hesitation about offering it. A good obstetrician would be a big help, however.

Dr Archie Duff was the answer—a calm, placid man, who never seemed fazed by even the most unlikely event or dire emergency.

And so far the team of Shona, Barry, Jessica and Archie had kept her going. Jessica and Archie kept in regular contact and all was progressing normally. An amniocentisis was deemed too risky, but the scan hadn't shown any problems and Shona had eventually decided that she could stop worrying and enjoy, if that was the right word, her pregnancy.

As Jessica abruptly returned to the present she realised that Shona was obviously waiting for the answer to a question. Or the response to a comment. Or something.

'Sorry, Shona. I was just remembering when you told me you were pregnant.'

'And now I've only got seven weeks to go. I can hardly wait.'

'Excited?'

'Yes. And fed up carrying this lump about.' She patted her bulge. 'From the kicking he's going to be a footballer.'

'Maybe *she's* going to be a ballerina.'

'Or even vice versa!' Shona laughed, then sobered. 'As long as it's healthy.'

The moment of silence stretched as both women offered up a quick prayer for a healthy baby and a safe delivery.

'It's funny. I'm not scared of *having* the baby—at least not yet—even at my advanced age.' She grinned and added as an aside, 'I might be thirty-eight and having my first, but that's not as bad as Dr Forrester!' She stopped and considered for a moment. 'Maybe that's what did it! Maybe it's catching!'

'Maybe,' Jessica agreed on a laugh.

Shona Whyte regarded her thoughtfully for a moment. 'You want to be careful—maybe you'll catch it next!'

Jessica's laugh was slightly forced this time as a wash

of pale pink ran up under her skin. 'Oh, I don't think there's much chance of that.'

'Well, you don't want to leave it too long!' came the advice that Jessica could well have done without. She could hardly tell a pregnant woman, let alone one who was a patient, that at the moment her career was far too important to her for her even to want to think about having a baby. Even if there were anyone suitable to be the father, that was! And since there wasn't, and it didn't look as though there would be. . . Shaking her head, she put her personal concerns on one side and forced her attention back to the woman in front of her.

The conversation she had had with Mrs Whyte about not leaving children too late came back to haunt Jessica's troubled dreams that night. She was quite happy as she was and wasn't looking to rush into marriage and a family. Not that she had anything particularly against the idea; it was just that her job seemed to take up most of her time and she was all too aware of friends getting side-tracked from their careers because their husband's career was put first and small children didn't sit easily with continued study and staying on the fast track. She knew she was doing well, that she was impressing the right people and that she could hope for a consultant's post at a reasonably young age, and she wasn't sure that she wanted to give up a glittering career to run around after some man. All of which made it very difficult to answer the question of why her dreams that night should be peopled with vivid images of a blond-haired, square-jawed giant and less distinct pictures of several small children—all with blond hair and vivid blue eyes.

The memories of her dreams haunted her the next morning and, try as she might, Jessica could not put them totally out of her mind. It had been a couple of weeks since her rescue by her shining knight and she was mildly concerned by how much he had wound his way into her thoughts. True, he had been very good-looking and overwhelmingly male, but since she wasn't usually attracted to the arrogant, macho type—and he had displayed characteristics of both—she still couldn't understand the unwelcome, unwanted attraction. Maybe it was the fact that he was unavailable, that she was never going to see him again, that made him a comfortable target for vague dreams.

Then there was the question of why she hadn't mentioned him to anyone. Normally her escapades—and it had to be admitted there were quite a few—were relayed to anyone who would listen. If they were sometimes embroidered a little on the way it was always to make the story funnier or more dramatic, and herself less competent, more accident-prone than she really was. Carless, she had had to admit problems and abandoning the car on her journey, and that she had been given a lift by 'some guy', but that had been it. No one had questioned her further, secure in the knowledge that if anything exciting or even halfway out of the ordinary had happened she would have told them. She didn't want to ask herself why she had chosen to remain silent about this particular adventure, which would have made such a good story against herself.

'Right, that seems reasonable.' Val wriggled in her chair and eased her position, one hand rubbing the small of her back as she agreed Jessica's plans for rearranging some of the groups which were run in the day hospital.

Collecting her things together, Jessica gave her boss a quick assessing glance. She didn't look well, her face drawn and her skin a pale, sickly colour with a greyish tinge. She had tried to say something but had been waved into silence by an unusually short-tempered Val, and so now kept her own counsel.

'There's one more thing. Before I tell the others tomorrow, Lizbeth Morgan, who was coming here as locum while I'm on maternity leave, can't come now. Something about her husband being posted abroad and she's going with him.' Val sniffed inelegantly and Jessica wasn't sure whether it was the lack of consideration Liz's husband had shown in having a job which sent him off to all parts of the globe at short warning or at Liz herself for so happily following him. 'Anyway, it's not the end of the world. An old friend is just back from a year in the States and more than happy to fill in until he takes up a new post at the university. Mike will—' Whatever she had been going to say was abruptly curtailed by a sudden gasp of pain as she lurched forward, clutching the edge of her desk.

All thoughts of locums and husbands being sent abroad fled Jessica's mind as she rushed to her friend's aid. Val quickly regained her control and insisted that she was all right, although she did relent enough to allow Jessica to help her down to her car as she agreed to go home.

The general hubbub in the staffroom was louder than usual. The day before there had been general agreement, from patients as well as staff, to go ahead with Jessica's plan for an art exhibition. Now that the decision had been taken enthusiasm was running high, although there was a fair amount of disagreement about the next step to take. The ringing of the phone was largely overlooked by most of those present and it was left to Naomi to answer it. So taken up were they with their heated conversation that it took a few minutes for them to realise that Naomi was talking in subdued tones, her pale eyes bright with unshed tears. As she was normally totally calm, unflappable, and not given to showing her emotions, the sight of Naomi almost crying was enough to bring swift silence to the room as they waited, mesmerised, to hear the bad news. For Naomi to react so overtly they had no doubt that the news was very bad indeed.

'Val?' Jessica guessed, putting all their worst fears into words.

Naomi nodded. 'She's been rushed into hospital with bleeding. It doesn't look too good. That was John.' She nodded at the phone, naming Val's husband.

'And the baby?'

With a shrug, Naomi blinked back tears. 'Hanging on. We can only hope. . .'

'And pray,' Sally, the student nurse, added and they all nodded.

'What are we going to tell the patients?' Graham broached the question which at least served to take their minds off their immediate feelings as they concocted a story which had enough of the truth in it not to mislead, but not enough to upset or worry them more than was necessary.

'Presumably Liz Morgan will take over sooner now?' Stuart asked, looking to Jessica for confirmation.

Realising that the rest of the staff did not know of the change of plans, Jessica heaved a heavy sigh and plunged into another explanation of yet more bad news. Liz was known to all of them and there had been no qualms about her taking Val's place. They all knew they could work with her.

'And who's this new person?' Naomi demanded, her belligerence a cover for her still not quite in control emotions.

Racking her brains, Jessica couldn't remember if Val had told her or not and eventually shrugged. 'It's a man; that's all I can remember. That, and the fact that if Val is prepared to call him a friend he can't be all bad!' Her comment lightened the mood as she had hoped and they all trooped out of the staffroom to confront the coming day as best they could.

'Someone will be along to take over next week,' Jessica told the rest of the staff at lunchtime. Most of her morning had been taken up on the phone to hospital administration and the clinical services manager trying to sort something out. 'We'll have to cancel Val's clinics for the next couple of days. I'll take emergencies until we know what is happening. I can always phone for help or advice if I need it.'

'Aren't you going off to a conference tomorrow?' Graham asked, causing a slight frown to crease Jessica's forehead. She was coming to think that Graham was taking altogether too much interest in her comings and goings.

'Yes, but I needn't fly down until tomorrow night. The conference starts Friday. Tomorrow was just going to be a holiday. I can cancel that.' She sighed inwardly. She had been looking forward to seeing her oldest friend, Jo, and catching up on news. Still, she could always visit her for a while in the evening.

* * *

It was much, much later than she had intended when Jessica got back to the hotel where the conference was being held. She had gone to Jo's for a late dinner and they had sat around giggling and gossiping, as they always did, while Jo's husband had cleared away the dinner and done the washing-up. Jessica envied Jo her husband, Bob, who always seemed ready to take a hand in the domestic chores and took an equal share in the raising of their two children. All the men she knew were too dominated by their ambition and wedded to their careers to want to take on such a role. But Bob was no slouch in the career stakes, if it came to that, holding down a demanding job in a City stockbroker firm.

It was with a sudden yelp of surprise that Jessica had noticed the time, leaping to her feet and rummaging around for her shoes which she had discarded some time earlier. Hearing the commotion, Bob had sauntered in from the kitchen, grinning.

'Just noticed the time, have you?' he enquired with a deceptively innocent air.

'I'll never make the last train,' Jessica wailed, only able to locate one shoe.

'That's the trouble with you girls—gossiping away, paying no attention to the time——'

'Why didn't you say something?' Jessica moaned, cramming her foot into the wayward shoe, only to discover it was one of Jo's and several sizes too small.

'Couldn't get a word in edgewise,' Bob reported solemnly, his mouth set firm but his dark eyes alight with laughter. 'Wouldn't have dared interrupt, either.' He sighed heavily and Jessica knew a moment's desire to heave her finally retrieved shoe at him.

Jo, however, sat placidly, watching her husband

teasing her friend, trusting him to have a solution but thinking she should help out.

'You can stay here——' she began, only to be cut off by Jessica.

'That's very kind, but I'd rather get back if I could. If I hurry I'll just make the train and——'

'You'll never make it,' Bob predicted, his suppressed smirk coming to the fore.

'Oh!' Jessica sat down, deflated. Nice as it would be to stay, she would rather be at the hotel. The conference started at nine a.m. prompt, and she wanted to look over her paper again. Now she would have to be up at the crack of dawn to get in, change into her suit and sort herself out. She was already nervous about the paper she was giving and had been hoping for a quiet, controlled start to the day.

Bob finally relented, seeing how genuinely worried Jessica looked. 'It's OK. I'll drive you back when you want to go.'

Jessica looked up at him smiling but simultaneously shaking her head. 'It's really kind of you, but I couldn't put you to all that trouble.'

'No trouble. It won't take long at this time of night and it's mayhem here in the mornings with the twins. You'd be better off at the hotel.'

'But——' began his wife, only to have Bob interrupt again, his smirk growing wider and more self-satisfied.

'If you're going to say, You've been drinking, I should point out I only had one glass of wine at dinner.' He sighed melodramatically. 'I *knew* this would happen and some of us think ahead and prepare.' His grin threatened to split his handsome face.

Rushing to him, Jessica hugged him, planting a grateful kiss on his cheek. 'Bob, you're wonderful.'

'Yes, I am, aren't I?' he agreed, clearly believing it was game, set and match to the male sex.

Jo came to thread her arm through his, kissing him on the other cheek. 'Wonderful,' she murmured ruefully. 'Any more perfect and you'd be totally insufferable.'

'But not tonight?' he enquired, his smug expression not changing by a fraction.

'No, not tonight,' his wife agreed softly. Then, in a firmer tone of voice, 'Now, make us some more coffee while you're being so saintly and leave us to finish our chat in peace.'

'Certainly, ma'am!' And, with a gently condescending slap to both their bottoms, he made a hasty exit before either of the two surprised women could retaliate.

Thus, it was nearly two o'clock in the morning when Jessica found herself outside her hotel-room door with a key which refused to turn in the lock. The bellboy had unlocked the door when she had arrived and he hadn't had any difficulty. Carefully she withdrew it from the lock and prepared to try again. Every sound was magnified in the silent corridor and she was overly conscious of the noise she was making. No matter how quiet she tried to be the key knocked against the tag — she banged the key against the keyhole trying to insert it and the doorknob rattled as she tried to turn it. Little sounds that by day would have passed unnoticed, in the early hours of the morning sounded as loud as bombs exploding.

Maybe it was the wrong key. She checked the number. It was the right key. There's a knack to this, she told herself. I can't *not* be able to unlock a door. This time, in her efforts to move silently, she dropped the key—which clattered on its descent to land with a soft thud on the deep-pile carpet. Her, 'Damn,' was muttered softly under her breath. One more time, she insisted, before giving in. She knew the look she would get if she went down to the reception desk and confessed herself unable to get into her own room. Stealthily she inserted the key—hitting it against the keyhole. Carefully she tried to turn it—the tag banged against the door, and once more she felt the resistance of the lock. Pulling the offending key from the lock, she began to straighten and became aware of a sound behind her—a sound not of her own making.

Turning, and still semi-crouched from her position at the door, she was confronted by a male torso inadequately covered by the white towelling robe supplied by the hotel. Belted tightly round the waist, it parted over a broad, tanned chest, liberally sprinkled with fine blond hairs. Feeling her mouth go dry, Jessica straightened up and encountered an uncompromising chin, a determined nose and a pair of vivid blue eyes, their expression one of long-suffering resignation. As their eyes met the expression in the blue ones changed to one if not quite of anger, then certainly of irritation. And was that distaste?

Without a word he took the offending key from Jessica's unresisting hand and stepped forward towards the door. Totally bereft of speech, she could only watch Michael Knight fit the key, silently, into the lock and, with one flick of his wrist, turn it and push open the door. Still silently he removed the key, put it in her hand and, giving her another penetrating glare, stalked back towards his own room. Gazing after him, Jessica had a splendid view of his long, bare legs beneath his robe, leading her to the intimate knowledge that he slept naked.

As that piece of information penetrated her numbed brain Jessica came back to life with a suddenness which unfortunately caused her to lose her grip on her handbag. In something like slow motion she watched the bag fall, its flap opening and the detritus of its contents spilling in an untidy mess across the carpet. Whether it was the thud of the bag or her strangled cry of horror Jessica didn't know, but something made the silent man turn round.

His eyes swept over her and the confused mess of make-up, hankies, diary, pens, perfume, keys, comb, and other assorted necessities of life strewn at her feet. His expression never wavering, he simply turned on one bare heel and walked through his door, closing it gently and silently behind him.

Half an hour later, totally unable to sleep, Jessica stared into the darkness. What was he doing here? She shied away from the obvious answer, reluctant to accept it. Eventually she relented. He must be a psychiatrist and here for the conference. She already knew he was a doctor and anything else would be even more of a coincidence, and too great to contemplate. The question which filled her mind, however, was did he recognise her? If he did, why didn't he say anything? Was he *so* horrified to meet her again? And if he didn't, what did that say about her impact on—it had to be said—a devastatingly attractive man? Her mind conjured up the memory of his bare chest and legs while her overactive imagination insisted on supplying details of the parts of his body which had remained discreetly covered. With a muffled exclamation of frustration, she rolled over in bed and forced her mind back to the original question. Did he, or did he not, recognise her? And, given his lack of response, what was the best answer? She fell asleep while trying to find one which wasn't wholly depressing.

His towering presence was in evidence the next day and he was totally unmistakable, standing head and shoulders above almost everyone else in the room. Their eyes met once, or at least Jessica thought they did, but since he didn't give a flicker of response she concluded it had been wishful thinking on her part.

She sat through his paper on the new drug Clozapine and noted that he was attached to one of the big American medical schools. Despite the paper being interesting and well-presented, with no waffle or unnecessary padding, Jessica realised that she was paying more attention to the warm bass voice than the content. A ripple of laughter ran through the hall at one point, starting her out of her daydream. It came as something of a surprise that he should crack a joke. Nothing in his demeanour so far had led her to believe that he was anything other than sober and rather forbidding. The good-humoured way he handled the questions was another eye-opener for Jessica. He was displaying a charm and lightness she would never have believed of him. Fleetingly she remembered that he had taken the time to charm Mrs Gordon at the village hotel. Maybe it's just me, she mused, who causes him to lose his charm.

And that was a less than cheering thought.

CHAPTER THREE

SLEEPING late was almost unheard of for Jessica and today of all days, when the new locum was starting, was a bad omen. She remembered the last time she had overslept and how that had led to her getting caught in a snowstorm. And being rescued. Twice in as many months was getting to be frequent! A vivid dream had awoken her in the middle of the night with a mild panic attack and, though she had resolutely tried to push it from her mind, it wouldn't disappear. It had taken ages to get back to sleep, hence her tardy wakening.

Rushing round her flat, grabbing at toast with one hand while trying to don her very professional-looking garb of navy blue suit with the other, she caught sight of herself in the mirror. Her dark brown naturally curly hair was in desperate need of cutting and, rather than framing her face with a controlled halo of curls, it now fell nearly to her shoulders in a wild mass of waves and curls which, although very attractive, did nothing for her image as a cool professional. There was nothing she could do about it now. But it was a bad time to look so feminine and abandoned. She remembered the nightmare, but refused to allow the images from her dream to surface. It couldn't be true. She wouldn't *let* it be true.

Leaving her car untidily parked in a spot which clearly said 'ambulances only', she rushed up the few steps into the building that housed the day hospital, hurtled past a surprised Janet at Reception and took the stairs to her office two at a time, her skirt riding high up shapely thighs to accomodate her stride. Afterwards she had to acknowledge that she wasn't looking where she was going, but it was still a surprise to encounter a wall where there shouldn't have been a wall as she reached the top. It was only when the wall produced an arm which gripped her own more than firmly, hauling her forward and preventing the force of the ricochet from hurling her backwards down the same stairs, that she felt the warmth of living flesh under her hands. Knowing what she was going to see when she looked up, and wishing it could be different, she nevertheless forced her head up and willed her breathing to slow down as her warm brown eyes met the dark blue of a frozen night sky.

'You!' Hadn't she known it would be? At some point during the night all the little clues—Val's mention of Mike, his time in the States—had come together in her nightmare which had Dr Michael Knight as the new locum consultant at the day hospital.

'Yes.' There was a flicker of something in his eyes, but otherwise his lack of response confirmed for Jessica that he too had worked out who she was. And wasn't best pleased, by the look of him.

Satisfying himself that she was securely balanced on her own feet, in as far as three-inch heels contributed to her balance, Michael Knight let go of her and moved back a pace. His eyes ran down the length of her body, pausing briefly on her heaving breasts as she regained her breath and frowning slightly as they reached her legs, her skirt still being caught up higher than propriety demanded from her inelegant run up the stairs.

As he let go of her Jessica found breathing easier and his overwhelming presence seemed less oppressive, although the look in his eyes was anything but reassuring. At five feet ten, with a penchant for high heels, she was used to towering over friends, colleagues and patients alike. No matter how high her shoes she would never come close to meeting the height of this man. It was a wonderfully comforting feeling.

In view of their previous meetings being less than positive, Jessica decided to try an upbeat approach and see if that would bring a lightening to his rather formidable expression. Her smile alone could usually win round the hardest heart.

'I'm terribly sorry I'm a bit late. I overslept. It's not like me to but. . .' Her voice trailed away and her bright, hundred-watt smile dimmed as she realised Michael Knight was not responding to her blast of practised charm. Used to charming her way out of most situations from a very young age, Jessica was thrown to find it not working on this particular man. A light flush of rose stained her cheeks as he continued to stare at her for a moment before he turned away.

'The staff meeting is just about to start,' he informed her coolly, already walking down the corridor to the staffroom.

He's got a twin! It was the only way she had of reconciling the laughing blond giant with the sparkling eyes now joining her colleagues with the hard-faced, cold-eyed man who had looked down his well-shaped nose at her a few minutes previously.

'Ah, Jessie.' Stuart caught sight of her and leapt to perform introductions. 'Dr Knight, have you met Jessica Balfour, the senior registrar?' His tone was more than slightly patronising and Jessica bristled with indignation. With all eyes on her, however, she had no option but to move forward and offer her new boss her hand. With barely a pause Michael Knight took it, engulfing it in his own enormous one, and smiled briefly at her and more fully at the gathered staff.

'We've met,' he informed them succinctly, and Jessica's heart sank. What on earth was he going to tell them? 'We—er—introduced ourselves at the conference on Friday,' he added, by way of explanation, granting him head-nods and smiles all round—except for a quick, hastily hidden frown from Stuart.

'Did Jessie describe the set-up to you, sir?' Stuart asked, taking a cup of coffee from Naomi's hands to pass it on to his boss.

'Thanks.' Mike smiled and Jessica was ridiculously pleased to see his appreciation was directed more to Naomi than to Stuart. Something was up with Stuart this morning; he didn't usually act like this.

'Our meeting was...fleeting,' Mike acknowledged on a rueful smile. 'We didn't get a chance to exchange any information.'

No, because you turned your back on me, Jessica thought wrathfully, then remembered the circumstances and blushed anew. Not because of her clumsiness at the encounter but because she vividly recalled what Dr Michael Knight had been wearing—or *not* wearing—and the broad expanse of his muscled chest with its tangle of blond hair. It wasn't usual to start a working relationship with such very personal knowledge and Jessica fought hard to replace it with a more circumspect image. As she looked away and sought to hide her confusion she noticed Stuart's assessing gaze on her and a very strange expression on his face. What *was* the matter with him?

All the patient notes were up to date and it didn't take them long to fill Mike in on the day hospital's routine. A brief overview of the patients was all that was feasible in the time, and Mike pointed out that he'd never remember all the details anyway and it was better that he get to know them over the next few days as individuals. For the moment, potential problems were the only things to be outlined. The meeting was just finishing when Stuart stopped them all in their tracks.

'There's one thing no one's thought to tell you, sir,' he said on a heavy sigh, as though he was going to do his duty even if it caused him pain, 'and I'm not sure how you're going to feel about it.' His tone indicated that he very much hoped Michael Knight *wouldn't* like what he was about to learn.

The consultant slumped back down in his seat, allowing the files he'd just gathered together to spill across the coffee-table. 'Well?' he demanded, almost irritably, when Stuart held his dramatic pause a moment too long.

Everyone else had stopped where they were at Stuart's announcement and were all looking at him with various degrees of surprise and impatience. With a premonition of disaster, Jessica suddenly realised what Stuart was about to say.

The younger man looked almost spitefully at Jessica, then turned to fill his new boss in on 'our Jessie's wee idea'. Although he did his best to make it sound as though they were all humouring her, Jessica was relieved at one point when Naomi, clearly unable to stand the patronising tone any more, butted in with a supportive comment of her own. She was vigorously supported by Graham and the nursing students. Stuart was not to be put off his stride, however, and came back, only to find Michael Knight glancing pointedly at his watch.

'I think I've got the general idea. I can find out the details later.'

'There's an exhibition committee meeting Wednesday lunchtime,' Naomi informed him, darting a scowl at Stuart when she thought no one was looking.

Jessica saw her and grinned her thanks for the support, then realised that Dr Knight had observed the exchange. And didn't look at all pleased by it.

Stuart made a last-ditch attempt. 'It wouldn't be too late to cancel, sir, if you wanted.'

'*What?*' Everybody in the room but Dr Knight and Stuart uttered the word in various tones of outrage, horror and sheer disbelief.

Michael Knight raised the more arched of his unusual brows and let a rueful smile play across his lips. 'It would seem that, were I to take such a very rash action on my first day here, I would risk alienating the entire staff. Not a good move, you must agree?'

Stuart's freckled skin flushed a fiery red to compete with his sandy hair. 'Well. . .'

But he was not to be let off lightly. 'Anyway, I think it is an excellent idea and Jessica should be congratulated on initiating it.'

For the first time Jessica knew what it was like to be on the receiving end of one of his smiles. A smile that did not merely show white teeth but that gleamed in the violet depths of his navy blue eyes, lines fanning from their corners to captivate her utterly. Now she knew what the word charm really meant. It was all the clichéd things she had ever heard—from the sun coming out from behind a cloud to hearing the first cuckoo of spring. So caught up in its warmth was she that it took several seconds for the surprise to register. She wouldn't have laid a bet on his supporting her. And now this. Maybe he was willing to let bygones be just that.

'Now it's time I did a tour of the place, I think,' Michael said casually, turning from her to collect his files once more. 'Maybe you could show me round, Jessica?'

It might be phrased like a question, but Jessica knew that it wasn't. With a mental sigh in the direction of the work piled up on her desk, she smiled brightly, 'Certainly—er——' What to call him? The hospital had a very informal feel to it, and it was an atmosphere Val had worked hard to develop. She knew that Stuart had found it a bit difficult to get used to when he had first arrived, just as he had been very reluctant to give up his white coat, but she'd thought he had adjusted. Apparently not. One sighting of a male authority figure and he was tripping over himself with the 'sirs'.

Dr Knight seemed to read her dilemma. 'I answer to Michael or Mike. Only my mother would dare try Micky.' There was a studied pause. 'And get away with it.'

Relieved laughter greeted this remark and the tense atmosphere lightened. As no doubt he had intended it to, Jessica thought, eyeing him covertly. She suddenly had the sense that he was very much in control and that for all his relaxed air nothing would escape his eagle attention.

'Five minutes, in my office.' He nodded at Jessica and headed out of the staff-room, leaving a rather dazed group behind him.

'Wow!' It took Sally, one of the students, to put

their feelings into words—even if they didn't all mean it in quite the same way!

'If I weren't happily married. . .' Naomi laughed.

'And ten years younger,' Graham said, so straight-faced and reasonably that he had Naomi nodding in agreement before the insult registered.

'Wretch!' She laughed at him. 'Just because you're still a wee babbie and wet behind the ears. . .'

Jessica left them to it, satisfied that the tension stirred up by Stuart had dissipated, and headed towards her room. She had a sudden urgent need to check her make-up before meeting with the consultant. Something that had never seemed necessary before her meetings with Val Forrester.

The day hospital was sited in a smallish two-storey, L-shaped building which had once housed a children's clinic. Both floors had a corridor running the length of the front of the building from which all the rooms led. As Jessica and Mike started down it she noticed that they were getting some openly interested stares from the few patients in evidence. Something would have to be done about introducing him to as many of them as possible, as soon as possible. One obviously felt the same way. Maggie, a long-time patient, hurried up to stand in front of them so that they had no option but to stop or rudely walk around her.

'Hello.' Michael Knight took the initiative before Jessica could say anything.

'You the new doctor?' Maggie looked very suspicious, gazing up at his awesome height from her slightly bent frame.

'That's right. I'm Michael Knight. And you are. . .?'

'Maggie.'

'Pleased to meet you, Maggie,' he offered, shaking

her hand, which had Maggie turning pink with pleasure.

'You're a big lad,' she observed, head thrown back as she stared openly upwards. 'I'm thinking you're even taller than Dr Pride.' She sounded accusing.

'Er. . .yes, just a fraction,' agreed Mike, writing off what was a good two inches.

'You're good-looking as well,' she observed blithely, adding for good measure, 'If you like blonds, that is.'

Jessica almost choked at that and noticed that even the urbane Dr Knight was having trouble controlling his expression. Maggie was sometimes worth her weight in gold!

'Thank you.' Mike accepted the compliment when Maggie appeared to be waiting for something.

The dumpy woman nodded her head and, as suddenly as she had stopped them, walked off. They could hear her muttering under her breath something about dark hair and brown eyes.

'Dr Pride is something of a favourite with Maggie,' she informed him needlessly.

'So I gathered. Tall, dark and handsome. I hope someone, somewhere will spare a kind thought for us poor blonds!'

About to say that he had absolutely nothing to be worried about and that she was sure he was knee-deep in admirers, Jessica found that the flippant words wouldn't come. Maybe it was just as well. She didn't really know him well enough yet to have that kind of teasing relationship, and she didn't want to cause him to retreat back into his formidable mode.

'What's going to be the best way of meeting the most patients at one time?'

'We could leave it until lunch, or see who's in the coffee-room now,' Jessica suggested.

But the coffee-room proved surprisingly empty and Mike merely briefly introduced himself to the few who were there.

Hughie shook Mike very firmly by the hand, staring hard into the younger man's face. A thick-set man in his forties, Hughie was nothing like as tall as Mike, but there was a menacing air about him. Or at least there was when he put his mind to it. Or when he was very ill. Everyone in the day hospital knew Hughie wouldn't intentionally hurt a fly. The defiant stare and squaring up to another male were simply standard behaviour in the part of the city in which he had grown up. Mike seemed to take it as such and calmly stood his ground, for which he got a reluctant grunt of approval from Hughie, who let go of his hand and shuffled back across the coffee-room to his abandoned cigarette.

'You don't implement the health board's no-smoking policy, then?' Mike asked conversationally.

Jessica glanced at him to see if he was serious and expected an answer. A bland face greeted her and so she shrugged lightly and turned away. The day hospital was exempt from the policy since it was recognised that a very high percentage of long-term psychiatric patients smoked and to get them to stop would be impossible. It was better to have them attend the hospital smoking than not have them come at all. Staff were not permitted to smoke, of course, but, Jessica thought ruefully as she contemplated the state of her lungs, there was no need. The amount taken in through passive smoking must be high indeed.

The top floor consisted of Val's office—now Mike's—with a magnificent view of the car park, and the room used by the senior registrar next door. The registrar's room was the other side. Next to them was the staffroom, with the large dining-room-cum-coffee-room running across the building at one end. There were also a number of other smaller rooms which were used for groups and various clinics. Downstairs were a number of consulting-rooms used by visiting staff, including other consultants, the psychologist and the social worker, more group rooms and the occupational therapy suite which included a kitchen, art-room, the OT's office and the relaxation-room, which had a pile of foam mattresses in one corner. Store-rooms, a shower-room, lavatories for staff and patients were dotted here and there wherever there was space for them. All in all, there was more to it than a casual glance from the outside would have indicated. Michael Knight seemed suitably impressed.

'I would have been to see it before I took up the locum,' he explained to Jessica, 'but with things working out the way they did. . .' He shrugged. There was nothing else to be said.

Val was improving, but wouldn't be back to work before the baby was born. That much Jessica knew, and she was damned if she was going to ask. If he couldn't understand how they all felt, and share whatever information he had, well, then. . . Her indignation must have shown on her face because Mike asked her if she was feeling all right before suggesting they go back to his office.

Lulled into a false sense of security by his affable manner throughout the quick guided tour, Jessica happily preceded Mike into his room and took the proffered seat, buoyed up with the notion that everything was going to work out between her and Michael Knight after all.

'What have you done to upset Stuart?'

His words caught her totally off guard and she could only splutter as she searched for an answer. As the silence stretched she felt the heat invading her cheeks, and knew that she must look guilty, although in reality she had committed no crime. What was going on? What did he mean?

When she didn't answer him immediately, Mike's frown deepened and he glared at her. 'Nothing to say?' His tone of voice was identical to the one he had used when he had hauled her so unceremoniously from her crashed vehicle.

Not liking to sound as though she was telling tales, Jessica nevertheless wasn't going to be cast as the 'baddie' when she had done nothing. Knowing attack was the best form of defence, she launched her first salvo.

'What makes you think I've done anything?' she demanded, and was gratified to see that the attack had caught Mike by surprise. He obviously hadn't expected her to take this line. 'I have done *nothing* to Stuart except be helpful when I could. If you're basing your conclusion on his little performance of this morning, then I'm as much at a loss as you are. He's never behaved like that before and I would have thought the attitude of the others there would have told you they were all equally surprised.'

'Hmm. Something, certainly, is going on.' Mike shot her another scowling glance from under heavy brows. 'Are you sure you don't know what it's about?'

'Certain!' As she spoke a tentative explanation

crossed Jessica's mind, causing her to sound less positive than she had intended.

The arching of Mike's brow while he leant back against his desk, his arms folded across his chest as he looked interrogatively at her, was as clear a non-verbal question as she had ever seen.

'Maybe it's you,' she began carefully, trying to think through the consequences of what she was about to say.

'You're suggesting he has something against me?' Mike sounded rightly astonished.

'No. Not at all. In fact, the reverse. I think he was trying to impress you.'

No response was probably the best she could have hoped for, Jessica thought as she became more convinced of her idea, but how much of it would she have to reveal? The very stillness of Mike emboldened her to continue. 'You're his new boss, after all, and it would be a natural desire. Maybe he thought you wouldn't like the exhibition idea.'

'Was he always negative about it?' Mike enquired, not giving any of his own thoughts away.

'No. Everyone was a bit surprised at first, but since then they've all been very enthusiastic. I think at Wednesday's meeting you'll find——'

Mike cut across her. 'Is that all you think it is?'

He was too perceptive by half! The first part of her theory she was sure was correct—this next part was very much more contentious.

'Well...there may be a bit more to it. The day hospital tends to be a bit, well, female-dominated,' she explained. 'I always thought that it didn't bother Stuart, but maybe I was wrong. I *do* think he wanted to impress you as his boss, but I also think he wanted to side with you as a man.'

Jessica wasn't sure what response she had expected to this idea, but Mike seemed monumentally unimpressed. Leaving his casually propped position on his desk, he moved to sit behind it, the gesture demonstrating an increased formality not lost on Jessica.

'That's quite a theory.' And one I don't think much of, his tone implied. 'Are you suggesting discrimination, or harassment, by any chance?'

'No, not at all.' Jessica could see that he didn't really understand what she was getting at. 'It's more a solidarity thing.'

'Hmm.' Mike seemed to give that some thought. 'Maybe he just thought you had bitten off more than you could chew with this exhibition and was trying to retrieve the situation before it was too late.'

'Maybe.' Jessica's expression gave the lie to her words. She *didn't* think that and knew that Mike knew she didn't. 'Everyone thinks——'

Once again he interrupted her. 'You seem to place a great reliance on "everyone".' He didn't try to hide the sarcasm this time. 'Judging by what I've seen of your abilities so far, I don't think *I'd* place too much reliance on your organisation skills. Do you always rely on other people to do your dirty work for you and get you out of trouble?' He sounded almost reasonable asking the outrageous question, and indignation led Jessica to rush into speech.

'That's not fair! Just because. . .' She tailed off. It would be hard to deny that he had met her twice and rescued her twice! That his intervention had been unasked for didn't negate his help. 'You haven't exactly seen me at my best,' she pointed out, accompanying the words with her most winning smile. A smile which appeared to have no effect on Dr Knight other than to deepen the frown which threatened to become a permanent feature on his handsome face.

'I've met women like you before,' he astonished her by saying. 'Oh, I'm not denying that you're probably bright enough and fairly competent at your job, but you go through life with the expectation that there will always be someone—some *man*—to pull you out of trouble. Is that what's happened with Stuart? Is that why he acted the way he did this morning?'

'That's an outrageous accusation!' Jessica leapt to her feet, her cheeks flushed and her breathing rapid. How dared he say such things? 'You have no right, no right at all——'

'Maybe, maybe not.' Mike seemed determined not to let her finish a sentence. 'Time will tell. And, for the moment, you're right—I shouldn't have made the accusation. So I'm sure you'll agree that your accusation against Stuart was also equally unfounded.'

He had her trapped. Damned if I do and damned if I don't, she thought to herself, and shrugged in agreement. 'You're right. I shouldn't have said anything.' And that much was true, no matter what else was or wasn't.

'Fine. I'll have a word with Stuart, too. One thing I won't have is backbiting by members of staff. The atmosphere carries over to the patients and won't do anybody any good.'

The strange interview was clearly at an end and as she returned to the privacy of her own office Jessica wondered how Michael Knight had managed, with so few words, to make her say something so indiscreet. Even if she was sure it was true, and by now she was, it should never have been mentioned. Somehow he had got to her, and she didn't like it! The second worrying aspect of the interview was his comments about 'women like her'. Had he been merely winding her up, getting her to realise how damaging an unthought-out accusation could be, or did he really mean it? And if he *did* mean it, then the future of their working life together didn't look too rosy. She sighed heavily and pushed her dark hair back from her face.

'I have to get it cut,' she muttered to herself as she vowed that for the duration of Dr Michael Knight's locum she would be the very model of organised efficiency. She would show him that she wasn't the half-wit he took her for and that she was nothing like the other dependent women he had known—assuming they weren't a figment of his imagination, of course! They were bound to be the glamorous, clinging type, she reasoned, unable to imagine him with anyone who wasn't stunning. And probably tiny, she thought despondently. I just hope he gets a bad back from stooping to kiss them. Then she wondered why she should even be thinking of his past girlfriends.

A knock at the door saved her from her muddled thoughts and she called out, 'Come in', with something like relief.

Jeannie MacPherson hovered at the door, looking, if anything, more anxious than usual.

'Jeannie. Come in. What can I do for you?' Jessica forced Michael Knight and his women to the back of her mind and focused on the thin, middle-aged woman still hovering at the door.

Jeannie took a step forward. 'It's about the exhibition, Doctor. I've had an idea.'

CHAPTER FOUR

'Come in, Jeannie. What's this idea?' Jessica smiled warmly at the older woman, coming round from behind her desk and indicating that she should take a seat in one of the comfortable chairs. At the back of her mind she noted that Jeannie had been content to say that she had had an idea and wondered if that wasn't a better way of starting than her own 'good idea'. She'd make a note of that for the future!

'Well, I'm not sure. . . Maybe I shouldn't. . .' Jeannie still hesitated in the doorway and Jessica tried again.

'I was just stopping for coffee. Would you like one?' she guided the woman to the chair and took the coffee from the stand where it had been filtering. Not for the first time she was grateful for a never-ending supply of coffee in her office. The purchase of the filter machine out of her own money had been well worth it.

Settled with a cup of coffee, Jeannie was still tongue-tied, and Jessica set about getting her idea out of her. She was impressed that Jeannie had got as far as coming to see her, let alone having 'an idea'. The woman was suffering from a depressive illness which had had strong obsessional characteristics. She was totally dominated by an elderly mother whom she cared for and who seemed to have whittled away all her confidence. Although she had been on medication for a while, they were now relying on a mixture of support and psychotherapy.

'Everyone's really taken with this exhibition idea, Doctor,' Jeannie began, sipping her coffee and refusing to meet Jessica's eyes.

'Good. I must admit when I first suggested it I did wonder if everybody would think it silly.'

It had been the right thing to say. Jeannie looked up, shocked. 'Silly! But you're a doctor!'

'And even doctors can have silly ideas.' Especially doctors, Jessica thought sourly, her mind on a certain very tall consultant. 'But I'm pleased it has gone down well.'

'Yes.'

It looked as though Jeannie wasn't going to say anything else and Jessica sought to draw her out. 'You said you had an idea. Are you going to do something for it?'

'Oh, no, Doctor.' Jeannie sounded petrified at the thought, then, as though girding her courage around her, she added, 'But I would like to help, though. Everyone is getting so enthusiastic about it. I'm not talented at all and I can't paint or do pottery or anything, but I did wonder. . .'

'Yes?'

'Well, you'll be needing someone to keep things in order and write letters and things, won't you? I could do that. I used to work in an office before I gave up to look after Mother and——'

She didn't get any further as Jessica leant forward and clasped her hands briefly. 'I think that's an absolutely wonderful idea! We certainly do need someone to take on the admin work. You're an absolute godsend!'

Looking startled at being so described, Jeannie

nevertheless brightened a bit. 'Well if you're sure. . . I might make a mistake. . .'

Jessica dismissed her worries. 'Everyone makes a mistake at some time. I'm sure you'll do really well and I can't tell you how much of a difference it will make. When do you want to start?'

Taking a deep breath, Jeannie plunged in. 'No time like the present. At least, that's what Mother always says.'

Jessica winked. 'For once she's right. We can work out a routine so you can use this office when I don't need it. I've sent letters to everybody I can think of asking them to bring the exhibition to the attention of patients, relatives and so on. An advert has gone off to several magazines for mental health groups and an artists' newsletter. I've already got some replies. They need filing and. . .' She stopped and waved her hands in the air. 'You'll see from the general mess that it all needs sorting out. I'll leave it to you to do what you think best.'

Jeannie looked at the pile of papers Jessica indicated that were spread over a chair and the floor in one corner of the room. 'Maybe if I take them away and look at them. . .?' she suggested.

'Great.' Jessica beamed at her, truly happy that such a timid woman had found the courage to make this suggestion. It might just be the best thing for her. 'We'll sort out later the best time for you to work, but if you find it getting too much for you, you only have to say.'

'Yes.' Jeannie sounded doubtful just for a moment, then brightened. 'If I'm left to myself, without anyone putting pressure on me, I'll probably do fine.' She gave a tremulous smile at Jessica, the first real smile Jessica could ever remember seeing from her. At that moment she knew that the exhibition really had been a good idea, no matter what anyone else thought.

'If you're sure. . .?' Mike Knight didn't sound quite as positive about it as Jessica had when she'd explained it to him.

'It could be just what she needs. Her mother has undermined all her confidence and this could give it back to her. It gives her a real job to do here; she'll feel useful——'

'Just as long as nothing goes wrong.'

Why was he being so negative? Jessica could feel her irritation mounting and strove to hide it from him. 'It won't. I'll keep an eye on her, but underneath that timid manner I think our Jeannie is a competent woman. It's just the depression which has taken the life, the confidence, out of her.' She grinned at Mike disarmingly. 'Anyway, bearing in mind her obsessive tendencies, I have little doubt that anything will go wrong. She'll check everything!'

Even Mike had to grin at that. 'As long as she doesn't overdo it and get anxious. . .'

'No. I really believe she's sensible enough and has enough insight to know when to stop.'

'OK. You've convinced me. We'll see how it goes.' His smile of approval lit his eyes, but somehow it only made Jessica more irritated.

'Right.' She wasn't used to having her every decision questioned and checked over. She had only mentioned this to Mike because it was slightly unusual and everyone would have to know anyway that Jeannie was doing the work. She hadn't expected to have to sell it to him as though his approval had to be especially won.

She was good at her job and knew what she was doing with Jeannie. Even in her enthusiasm for the exhibition she wouldn't compromise the care of any of her patients.

'The exhibition's going well, is it?' Mike asked and Jessica had the odd idea that he was trying to prolong their chat, rather than having any real desire to hear the answer.

'Yes.' She launched into a detailed account only to be brought up short by his sudden interruption.

'I'll get all the details at the meeting.'

Why did you ask, then? Jessica thought to herself, but wisely refrained from saying so aloud. But it seemed he wasn't finished with the subject. 'Are you putting any work in?'

The question caught her off guard and she looked astonished. 'Me? No. I can't paint.'

His eyes narrowed at that.

'Why?'

He shrugged. 'I wondered if painting was—er—your thing. If that was why you were interested.'

'No. It just seemed——' she grinned '—a good idea at the time.'

Of course he didn't get the joke and looked blankly at her. 'What are you getting out of it, then?'

She was incensed. 'Why do I have to get anything out of it? Why can't I just think it's a good thing to do?'

'It's a lot of extra work.'

'You don't have to be involved!'

Now it was his turn to look surprised. And offended. 'That wasn't what I meant at all. I just thought——' But Jessica wasn't to discover what it was that he thought. The phone sounded and without a pause Mike picked it up and Jessica fled from the room. Fortunately she had her outpatients waiting.

As she left Mike's office to turn into her room a movement at the end of the corridor caught her eye. Hughie was standing a few inches from the wall, rocking backwards and forwards on his heels. For a moment Jessica thought he was banging his head against the wall, then she realised that his hair was only brushing the wall and that he was doing no damage to himself. She approached slowly and became aware of the low chanting that was coming from him. The words were indistinct but he sounded angry and he gave absolutely no indication that he was aware of her presence. He hadn't been talking to his voices for some time now, although she knew they formed a fairly constant backing chorus to his life. It looked as though he was beginning to relapse. She would need to see him that afternoon and try to establish if anything out of the ordinary had happened to put him under additional stress. She knew it was well established that people with schizophrenia coped with stress less well than those who did not have the illness, and that unexpected pressures could bring about a relapse or exacerbation of acute symptoms. If that was what had happened with Hughie she would have to try to do something about it before his symptoms became even more florid and the relapse was well underway. Reviewing his medication would be a first step but by no means the whole story. Before she reached him, however, Graham appeared and apparently found nothing out of the ordinary in Hughie's behaviour as he approached him confidently, said a few quiet words to him and led him back into the therapy-room and group discussion. Making a mental note to talk to Graham later, she returned to her own room.

The Wednesday lunch-time exhibition meeting caused Mike some surprise as well. Jessica could see that by the narrowing of his eyes as his brows came together when a senior accountant from the sector walked in.

'Harry! What are you doing. . .?' He didn't finish the question as the older man pulled up a chair and joined the group.

'Keeping an eye on the money,' Harry told Mike, although that was fairly obvious. 'Jessica quite rightly didn't want to be responsible for the accounting and we have opened a special account for the art exhibition money. I'm dealing with it all.'

'Isn't it a bit small fry for someone in your position?' Mike asked the question unthinkingly and was rewarded by a snort of derision from Naomi, who was seated next to him. Harry Smith just grinned.

'Possibly. But it's fun!' That wasn't the answer Mike had expected from a senior accountant but by the grin on her face it *was* what Jessica had been waiting for. 'And it gets me away from the office for an hour.'

'How's the painting coming?' Jessica asked as she handed their 'financial adviser' a cup of coffee .

'Slowly. I could do with more time, but I'm really glad I picked up a brush again. It's years since I painted.'

'You're doing a painting for this exhibition?' Mike sounded truly astonished and Harry laughed at the younger man's expression.

'I think I might be calling it *Breakdown of a Manager*! It's about the frustrations of having to balance the books and run the service on too little money. . .' He trailed off. 'Not that I have to tell any of you about that.'

Mike still looked thunderstruck but by now everyone had arrived and got coffee, produced their sandwiches, and the meeting was ready to get underway. It was then, as she was about to call them to order, that Jessica realised Mike didn't have any lunch. Obviously no one had thought to tell him that they all brought their own sandwiches. Unobtrusively she pushed hers towards him. 'Have one of mine.'

'It's OK. I'll get some later.'

'They'll be sold out. Go on.' She didn't mind giving him a sandwich and thought, almost ruefully, that maybe this would be the only chance she would get to help him out.

As he picked one up, almost reluctantly, Mike turned and smiled his thanks at Jessica and she felt as though the floor had given way beneath her. Laughter-lines fanned round his eyes and there was a warmth in them that she had never seen before. As his sensuous lips curved upwards and his teeth flashed white her heart began thumping out a quickened rhythm in her chest and she knew she would give practically anything to see him go on smiling like that. At her. She couldn't look away and words just wouldn't come. It was Harry who broke the spell.

'Maybe we should get on, Jessie. I've to be back by half-past.'

The meeting went well and Jessica could see that Mike was impressed by the planning that had gone into the venture thus far, and by the money they had raised to support the exhibition.

'This is a much bigger project than I'd realised.' They were walking along the corridor from the meeting and the frown was back, creasing his forehead and making him look several years older than when he had smiled at her.

Jessica was immediately on the defensive. 'It's well in hand. I don't think they'll——'

He cut her off. 'I wasn't criticising,' he told her and although Jessica wanted to retort, Weren't you? she held her tongue. 'I was merely commenting. I think you're going to have to fill me in on all the details if I'm to understand everything that is going on.' He looked at his watch.

'You mean now?' She sounded confused. Surely they were both due at clinics.

'No, I don't mean now!' He sounded irritated—as though he expected her to read his mind, Jessica thought, irritated herself. 'You admitted this was an extra-curricular activity and I certainly haven't got time to discuss it during the day, even if you have. We had better meet one evening and you can give me the details over a drink.'

'If that's what you want.' That Jessica was surprised by his comment—it could hardly be called an invitation—was an understatement. The last thing she had expected from him was the suggestion of any sort of social contact. Nevertheless, she wasn't going to let him see that the idea of meeting him for a drink was exciting and something she would be looking forward to. That wouldn't do at all.

'What about tomorrow?' he said. Jessica nodded, knowing that she was going to agree to anything he suggested, but Mike was already frowning again. 'No, that's no good. I've got a date tomorrow. How about. . .? No. . .' He was so clearly searching his memory for a free evening that Jessica felt her heart plummet. It wasn't that she was surprised. A man who looked like Mike Knight would have women queueing up round the block just on the off-chance that he might be able to spare them some time. But it was depressing to have that so graphically brought home to her. What chance would she have?

The question stopped her in her tracks. What was she thinking of? She couldn't possibly be interested in Mike Knight. True, he was a devastatingly sexy man who only had to smile at her to turn her knees to jelly, but. . . But she wasn't interested. She didn't have time to be interested! Anyway, someone like Mike would expect a woman to have more time to give him than she had to spare on any man, at least for the next couple of years. *And* she wasn't about to join any queue of women. *And* she didn't believe in mixing work with personal relationships. It never worked. There were always problems, especially since he was her boss. That would be a disaster. No, she really wasn't interested in him. Aware that she was desperately scrabbling around for reasons to convince herself that she *wasn't*, was absolutely *in no way* interested in Mike, she also realised that he was waiting for the answer to a question she hadn't heard.

He was back to looking disapproving. 'I said is Monday all right?'

'Er. . .yes. . .yes. Fine. Great.' Shut up, Jessica, she told herself; you sound like a moron. Mike must have thought so too as he gave her a very odd look before swinging away into his office. At his door he turned back to her. 'By the way, I'll be away all day tomorrow and Friday. Meeting in Edinburgh.'

Letting out a sigh, Jessica escaped to her own office, dropping her pile of files on to her desk and collapsing in her chair. She ran her fingers through her hair, pushing it off her face—now coloured with the heat of embarrassment. He must wonder what the matter was with her. *She* wondered what the matter was with her. But she had until Monday to get some perspective on her thoughts about Dr Michael Knight.

As she turned back to her desk and set of patient files for the afternoon her hair swung round her face. I have to get this cut, she thought, for the umpteenth time.

She had been lucky. Geena, her hairdresser, had had a last-minute cancellation and was only too happy to fit Jessica in when she phoned on Friday. Now, first thing Saturday morning, she was sitting with her wet hair dripping round her face, drinking a much needed cup of coffee. She peered at herself in the mirror and wondered if hairdressers deliberately had mirrors that made you look washed out and five years older. She peered again. No, make that ten. It hadn't helped that she had spent too long reading a letter from Jo which had arrived in the morning mail and hadn't had time to put on any make-up. Not that it was important; she only had to dash back to her car, and she wasn't likely to see anyone here who mattered. She buried her nose back in the fragrant coffee and wondered where Geena had got to.

'Hello, Jessica. Fancy meeting you here!'

She blinked. It couldn't be. Life couldn't be that unfair—could it? It seemed it could. A body that dwarfed the chair, and made the towel round his shoulders look like little more than a facecloth, seated himself next to her, looking remarkably pleased to be seeing her. Jessica stifled her groan and tried, unsuccessfully, to smile in return.

'Hello, Mike. Yes, what a surprise.' The young assistant hovering by his side ran off to get his coffee and Jessica stared glumly ahead as a drip of water rolled slowly down her nose. How had she possibly missed seeing him come in? His blond hair looked very much darker when wet, but other than that the fact that his hair had just been washed and that he was draped in a robe that was too small, with a dark green towel round his shoulders, did nothing to detract from either his looks or his authority. Jessica stared at her reflection. She looked like a drowned rat. An old, colourless drowned rat.

Mike accepted his coffee from the girl with a smile that had her blushing to the roots of her cleverly tinted hair and that was the final straw as far as Jessica was concerned. She had never felt so much at a disadvantage with him. Well, not since. . .the last time. She sighed. Was he never to see her capable, confident, and done up to the nines? And, to add to her confusion, he seemed to find nothing odd in launching into a description of the meeting he had been at in Edinburgh. Vainly she tried to think of something sensible to say.

At that moment Geena bore down on Jessica, brandishing her scissors and almost taking off one of Jessica's ears as she caught sight of Mike.

'Hello, I'm Geena. You're new here aren't you?'

Jessica ground her teeth as she watched Mike turn on his most charming smile for the stunning blonde in the skin-tight Lycra skirt and shake her hand, introducing himself as he did so. She banged her empty coffee-cup down on the ledge in front of her with such a clatter that the other two turned to look at her with some surprise.

'Sorry, Jessie.' Geena smiled. 'I was just getting acquainted with a new client.'

'You'll lose an old one if I sit here dripping much longer,' Jessica mumbled, and knew that Mike had heard her when his grin deepened. 'I'll die of pneumonia,' she justified herself, but knew he knew what she had really been thinking.

'You'd better do whatever it is you're going to do to her hair,' Mike generously offered, with a nod at Jessica. 'She's not at her best in the mornings, is she?'

And that could be taken several ways, she realised as Geena gave her a very speculative look.

'Who is he?' Geena demanded, breathing the words into Jessica's ear as she leant forward to reach for her comb, but Jessica just shook her head. She wasn't about to discuss Mike Knight with Geena, particularly when he was sitting only a few feet away. Even after he had left all she would say was that he was someone she worked with.

They had met in passing first thing Monday morning and Jessica had been unsure how to respond to his laughing, 'Nice haircut,' as a finger had flicked one of her curls. Since then she hadn't seen him and now, reading the first words of the note Mike had left her, felt her heart sink. He couldn't make their drink that evening—some late meeting had come up. She read further and her heart took wings. They'd better eat instead. It was hardly an invitation to dinner but it did mean he wanted to. . . No, to see her wasn't what he wanted. What Dr Mike Knight wanted was to find out what was going on with the exhibition and how much it was going to continue to disrupt the day hospital. That was what this 'invitation' was about. He suggested that they meet at the restaurant. So much for wishful thinking that this was a date. She noted that the restaurant named was, nevertheless, eminently respectable and somewhat pricey. Well, that was up to him. She shrugged slim shoulders.

'What are you going to do about Hughie?' Graham stood in the doorway, a worried frown creasing his boyish face. 'He's going downhill.'

'Yes, I know.' Jessica threw down her pen on the desk with an air of frustration. Hughie wasn't responding to the increased medication and his behaviour was becoming more bizarre. With a gesture of weary defeat, she gestured for Graham to come in and sit down. 'Tell me about it.'

Which he did. Clearly and concisely. Hughie was again showing the signs of acute schizophrenia. He was obviously hearing voices—indeed, he was carrying on long conversations with them. He was becoming increasingly suspicious and paranoid and as a consequence was avoiding people because he thought they were trying to control him.

'I'll see him tomorrow and review his medication again,' Jessica promised.

'Do you think he needs to be admitted?' Graham asked, but Jessica shook her head.

'Not if we can help it. You know how much he hates coming in.'

'Yes, but he's getting very worked up about his neighbours again. He says he can hear them plotting against him through the wall.'

'Hmm.' Jessica remembered that there had been

trouble with the neighbours before. 'I'll talk to him tomorrow.'

'OK.' Graham hesitated.

'Anything else?' Jessica wanted to get back to her work and something of that must have got through to Graham as he reddened slightly, but shrugged. 'No. I'm off. Are you coming too?'

'No. I'll stay on a bit. I've got a lot of catching up to do.' She waved her hand at a pile of papers on her desk.

'Right. Goodnight.'

As she listened to Graham's footsteps clattering down the stairs she thought again of Hughie and sighed. She was running out of ideas.

Running her fingers through her now much neater bob of curls, Jessica stretched back in her chair to throw her arms wide before dropping them and shaking her hands. She had been sitting hunched over the computer for far too long. Everyone had gone home some time ago and she was making use of the quiet time to get some backlogged data from her research put on to the computer. They were engaged in an audit project, evaluating some of the day hospital's services against a set of external criteria. What they really needed was a good needs assessment, but Jessica knew they didn't have the resources for that. This was the best they were going to be able to do. Glancing at her watch, she decided it was about time to start packing up, to go and meet Mike at the restaurant, when she thought she heard a noise. Instantly she froze, holding her breath as though even the sound of her breathing would carry to an intruder. She had made sure all the outside doors were locked after the last person had left. How could anyone have got in?

Had someone stayed hidden after the day hospital closed and now come out? It didn't seem likely. Why would anyone want to do that? Her mind ran on, thinking of dangerous madmen, before she stopped her thoughts with a sense of shock. What on earth was she thinking of? Shouldn't she know better than most that the vast majority of people with a mental illness were *not* dangerous? The prowler was much more likely to be a youth on the look-out for a suitable target for mindless vandalism. That sounded nearly as prejudiced, she acknowledged, but, given the area the day hospital was situated in, it was also more probable.

There was nothing for it but to go and investigate. Whoever was walking up the stairs must be sure that there was no one in the building for he was not making any attempt to muffle his footsteps. Maybe she could stay hidden away here? That smacked too much of cowardice for Jessica and she set out. The footsteps had stopped and she wondered where the man—it had to be a man—had gone. Creeping to the top of the stairs, she held her breath and very cautiously peeped round.

'Aaah!' she screamed as she came face to face with a very surprised, handsome face.

'Aaah!' Mike yelled as he tottered on the steps before falling backwards.

'Ohh!' Jessica moaned as she realised who the intruder was and what had just happened to him.

'Ohh!' Mike groaned, and he rubbed the head that had broken his fall—by colliding with the wall—as he slid down that same wall to fall in a heap on the half-landing.

'Are you all right?' Jessica bounded down the stairs,

her fear of the intruder replaced by a new fear for Mike's safety.

The look he gave her said everything.

'Where does it hurt?' she enquired and only received a look more speaking than its predecessor.

Gingerly Mike heaved himself to his feet and it concerned Jessica that he didn't seem altogether steady. One hand was clamped to the back of his head.

'Here, let me help you.' She took a step towards him, hand outstretched, and was cut to the core when Mike took an involuntary step back.

'No, don't come near me. You've done more than enough already. *You*,' he spoke heavily, 'are nothing short of a walking disaster area.'

Jessica moved back to let him stagger past, picked up the briefcase which he had, not surprisingly, dropped in the fall and silently followed him upstairs. Her heart couldn't have sunk any lower and she thought that this time he really wouldn't forgive her. There didn't seem to be much point in reminding him that he had scared her just as much as she had scared him. By the time they reached the top of the stairs Jessica was relieved to see that his unsteady gait had improved and that not too much damage had been done. She recalled the force with which he had hit the wall. He must have one hell of a headache.

Mike reached his office with barely a stagger and Jessica put his briefcase well out of the way beside his desk. The last thing she needed now was for either of them to trip over that.

Mike sank down in his chair and shook his head forcefully, reminding Jessica of a bull she had once seen charge against a wall—and come off worst.

'How do you feel now?' she asked carefully, not

wanting to bring his wrath down on her head again. 'Do you think you should have an X-ray?'

The noise Mike made told her exactly what he thought of her idea and, no doubt, X-rays in general. In case she hadn't got the message, he spelt it out. 'No, I do not think I need an X-ray. And yes, just at the moment I feel foul and as though my head is going to drop off. Is that what you wanted to know or was there more? In fact, there is more. My ankle throbs.'

'I'm sorry. I didn't know it. . . What are you doing here anyway?'

'I just wanted to pop in and drop off some stuff before going to meet you at the restaurant——Look, just go away and leave me in peace before you do any more damage.'

Feeling there was no alternative, Jessica crept out of his office, wanting to do nothing so much as sit down and have a good cry. Instead she went into the common-room and made a cup of tea, taking it back to Mike with two paracetamol. When she entered his room he didn't move and it looked to her as though he hadn't moved since she had left. Silently she put the tea and pills on the desk in front of him and prepared to creep out again.

'Thank you.' That was more than she had expected from him and the two words gave her hope.

'Is it very bad?'

He shrugged, then winced. 'I'll live, if that's what you mean. And I won't bother to sue you!'

'Sue me?' Her voice rose a tone. 'What do you mean, sue me?'

'Aggravated assault.' He gave the ghost of a smile. 'Something like that. It sounds right anyway. You certainly are aggravating. And it was definitely assault. Creeping round the corner like that——'

Injured or not, she wasn't letting him get away with such outrageousness. 'Me! You were the one creeping about the place, scaring me half to death. If anyone is going to be sued, it should——'

'Jessica, shut up.' The words were said with a weary kind of patience as he stood up to face her, which only served to inflame Jessica's growing temper. That her anger was as much a result of fright as anything else she ignored. He wasn't going to talk to her like that. Who did he think he was?

'No. You're the one——'

Whatever else she had been going to say was lost as Mike reached for her and silenced her most effectively by covering her mouth with his own. As kisses went it started out as a means of silencing her from a man in pain, angry and frustrated, but within seconds it had turned into something else entirely. His lips, warmly soft at first, hardened as the caress deepened and his tongue slipped into her mouth to tease her own tongue into his.

Quite without her volition Jessica's hands had come up to rest on Mike's broad shoulders, and were now sliding along their well-muscled breadth to glide round his neck, while his hands had fastened round her waist and were pulling her against his chest. Tall as she was, Jessica felt totally dwarfed by him and at the same time protected by his size. As his tongue pushed its way between her lips and found the sensitive interior of her mouth her hand caressed the back of his head. And encountered a lump the size of an egg.

'Ouch!' He let go of her instantly and leapt back as

though shot. And, indeed, from the brief feel she had had of his injury, he would be in some pain from it.

'That's some lump! Are you sure you don't need it looked at?'

'Yes, I'm sure,' he growled, and Jessica's face flamed as she remembered just what they had been doing when she'd discovered the bump. She noted with some interest that Mike's colour was also slightly heightened as he mumbled, 'Sorry about that. Put it down to the bump on the head. And shock.'

'Er. . .yes.' She stumbled over the words, aware that she didn't want to dismiss it so prosaically. While it had lasted, the kiss had been quite something. Her close encounter with Mike had left her wanting more.

But Mike misinterpreted her response. 'You're quite right, of course. That's no excuse. I can only repeat, I really am sorry and I assure you that I don't normally go around grabbing women and forcing myself on them.' His colour was much darker now and Jessica sensed his acute embarrassment and sought to ease it.

'There's no need to apologise. I think we were both in shock. Let's just forget it, shall we?'

He nodded, then winced.

'I think you should go home. Would you like me to drive you?' The look of panic in his eyes caused her to continue without even missing a beat, 'No, on second thoughts, maybe we should get you a taxi. You're certainly in no state to drive yourself.'

And for once Mike didn't say a word.

CHAPTER FIVE

THE taxi drew up outside an impressive red sandstone tenement building in Glasgow's west end and almost despite herself, Jessica thrilled at discovering where Mike lived, at the anticipation of actually seeing his home. As they got out of the taxi she noticed that Mike still looked a trifle unsteady on his feet, but that didn't stop him protesting at her presence. He turned to pay the taxi driver and Jessica was dismayed to hear him say, 'Don't go—the lady isn't staying.'

Leaning past him and closing the door, Jessica told the bemused driver, 'It's OK. You go. I'll see him into his flat.'

'I've told you, I'm perfectly capable of looking after myself.' He opened the cab door and looked pointedly at her.

Smiling sweetly, Jessica moved to the open door and took the handle from him, making out that she was about to get in. As Mike moved back a pace to give her room she swung the door shut and turned back to him.

'And I think you need a check-up. I'm coming in.'

They stood glaring at each other while the taxi driver watched with growing interest and amusement.

'No. Take the taxi home, Jessica.'

'No. I'm going to make sure you're all right if it's the last thing I do.' She faced him belligerently and, despite his height and massive frame, Jessica's energy and determination for once seemed to dwarf him.

What would have happened next she had no idea, but the taxi driver had clearly had enough entertainment and decided that earning a living came before witnessing the minor dramas of other people's lives.

'I'd give in if I were you, mate.' He offered the advice cheerfully. 'It's always easiest in the long run.' And with a broad wink he set the cab in motion and left the two antagonists facing each other on the street. Both, for a second, were speechless.

Then, with a muttered exclamation of disgust, Mike turned and headed for the building, obviously having decided to take the unasked-for advice. Jessica followed him up to the third floor, but took the keys out of his hand when he had difficulty getting the key in the lock. Was that a bad sign? she wondered as he almost sagged against the door-frame. But once she had the door open he straightened, following her into his flat, suddenly looking very much better. Brushing past Jessica, he walked into the living-room, stopping to turn on a couple of lamps as he went to the wide windows and pulled heavy curtains across them, shutting out the winter darkness illuminated by the lights of the city nightscape. Turning back to Jessica, still standing uncertainly in the doorway, he asked smoothly, 'Now what?' one eyebrow raising in lazy enquiry.

Appalled, Jessica could feel the beginning of a tide of hot colour surging up her throat to tint her face, but she pretended that nothing was out of the ordinary, standing her ground as she glanced round the large room decorated in neutral tones of cream, beige, tan and dark brown. A very masculine room, she owned, with no concession to feminine taste at all.

The moment of space had calmed her, or so she

thought, but she still couldn't prevent her voice sounding slightly higher than normal. 'What, "now what"? I don't know what you mean.' Her mind flew back to the shared kiss. Did he think she wanted to take up where they had left off? That her body was screaming 'yes' she chose to ignore. Her mind was very firmly telling her it wasn't a good idea.

If anything, Mike's eyebrow went a fraction of an inch higher. 'Come now, you made enough of a fuss to get here—what do you want to do now? Do you want a drink?'

Striving for control, she took refuge in being a doctor. 'I don't think drinking is a very good idea,' she responded, outwardly calm. 'You should——'

'I wasn't intending to drink,' Mike broke in smoothly. 'Even I——' he laid heavy emphasis on the personal pronoun '—can see that that would be a stupid idea. I thought you were the one who could do with a drink. You're looking very——' he paused as though searching for a word '—het up about something.'

Taking a deep breath, Jessica worked hard on retaining her cool. 'I am not "het up", as you put it. Concerned, naturally——'

'Oh, *naturally*,' he echoed softly, but she ignored his interruption.

'—for your well-being, and no, I do not want a drink.'

'If you're sure. . .?'

'Yes, I am.'

Mike sighed, running fingers through his hair and wincing when he inadvertently touched his bump. 'What is it with you, Jessica?' he asked, sounding totally frustrated, a troubled expression clouding his navy eyes to black.

'What. . .? I don't know. . .' But, as though she hadn't spoken or he hadn't heard her, Mike turned his back on her and ran his hand across the back of his neck, as though to ease the tension.

'You always seem to be causing mayhem somewhere or to need rescuing from something, and yet. . .' His words trailed off and he pivoted back to face her. 'And yet you're not really helpless, are you?'

'No, no, I'm not.' Jessica kept her voice low, although something inside her wanted to shout the words at him. Don't see me as a liability, as a problem, she wanted to say, but the words wouldn't come. Perhaps it was just as well.

'I've had my fill of helpless women,' he was now saying, and Jessica had the uneasy feeling that he wasn't completely aware of what he was telling her, or even that she was there at all. 'With my name, I was bound to get teased about "knights to the rescue" and so on. And my size didn't help. I suppose I got fed up with it in the end, and with the stupid women who wanted a "hero". I always seemed to end up with girlfriends who were the clinging, helpless type. Or at least turned into that when they were with me. I always seemed to be rescuing them from their own folly; they saw me as the great protector and wanted me to prove it. I've been in a few fights in my time. There's something about drunks which makes them want to take on someone my size and I was always having to find ways out of difficult situations without actually hurting anybody.'

'I didn't realise.' Jessica's mind was rapidly reviewing what Mike was telling her, giving her a very different picture of him. Had she been guilty, like everyone else, of simply seeing him as a rock on whom she could lean? And how uncomfortable it would be to be that rock.

'Then there was the business of Nathan Pride's wife.'

'What?' Jessica sat up straighter at that. She had met Rowan Stewart on several occasions and liked her. What had gone on between her and Mike? Something of what she was thinking must have shown on her face because Mike hastened to set her right.

'No, nothing like that. There was some trouble with a couple of boys. This was before they were married, of course, and I was Nathan's senior registrar. Anyway, the two of us waded into the fray and rescued Rowan and a patient she was with. Nathan was the one who did all the fighting. I just phoned for the police but, of course, the story grew in the telling and inevitably it was back to "knight to the rescue". And then the girl I was seeing at the time got jealous and deliberately set up a scene up in a pub so that I had to launch in and protect her, getting a black eye in the process. After that I vowed there would be no more helpless females.'

'Ah!' Light had finally dawned. Mike saw her as one of those self same 'helpless females' and that was why he was fighting the attraction. But she wasn't helpless. She was a competent professional. She would just have to convince Mike of it. But not now.

The silence stretched tautly and with an embarrassed cough Mike broke it. 'Maybe I shouldn't have said so much.'

'No,' she countered swiftly. 'I understand.' There was a painful pause and Jessica knew that she had to change the subject. 'We were going to talk about the exhibition but I don't think now is a good time. The best place for you is bed.' As the words left her mouth she realised that the sentiment could have been worded better. She *did* think Mike should be in bed—resting—but, the mood he was in, he was likely to put another interpretation on it. She blushed for the third time in what seemed a few minutes, averted her eyes from his handsome face and waited for Mike's comments. When none came she risked a quick look at him and was surprised to find him watching her with an almost detached calculation, although one eyebrow was, inevitably, quizzically raised.

All he said was, 'You're probably right,' in such a neutral tone of voice that she could only stare.

'Right, then. . .if you're really OK. . .' Suddenly she couldn't wait to get out of his flat, away from the strange expression on his face. An expression that was almost too knowing, almost too. . . 'Right,' she repeated herself and backed out of the door. 'I'll see myself out.' And before Mike could say anything more she took to her heels and practically ran from the room, from the flat, from Mike.

Fortunately, in that part of the city, there were always a lot of cruising taxis and a minute later she was huddled in the corner of a black cab being borne back to her own flat, where she hoped she would be able to block out the events of the evening. She was beginning to think Mike would never see her as anything other than a walking disaster area and that was a pity. Not that she wanted. . . She stopped. She didn't really have any idea what she did or didn't want. She was attracted to Mike, that much was certain. But there was no need to do anything about it. Mike was an attractive man. That was all there was to it. She was responding like a normal female. No big deal.

What she wanted—needed—was for him to see her as a competent professional woman, someone he would support in her career. Jessica knew that she was good at her job and had no real doubts about her capabilities. It was just this unfortunate habit she had of getting herself into scrapes. On the whole it amused people rather than angered them—or so she had believed. After what Mike had said this evening, though, she was having second thoughts. Did it make people wary of trusting her? Would they see her as a candidate for a consultant's post or would they see her as a rather amusing lightweight? Did it mean she would have to keep proving herself?

Surely her slightly scatter-brained image hadn't done her any harm up to now, had it? She hadn't done anything serious and never anything to compromise a patient. So why was she still worried? And she was. She couldn't deny it any longer. Her mind backtracked. People were amused. Mike was angry. Mike didn't want anything more to do with her than he absolutely had to.

Mike was the only person to respond with anger. Was it the anger which was disturbing or the fact that it was *Mike* who was angry? If she was going to be honest with herself—and what had she got to lose by that?—then she had to accept that it was Mike's reaction that was bugging her, and had been since their first meeting. Without conceit she knew that she was pretty—pretty rather than beautiful—but that her liveliness, her vivacity gave her an additional attractiveness which drew people to her. It wasn't just men, but women and children, too—although her charm was most potent on men. And here was Mike, the most attractive man she had met in a long while, who refused to succumb totally to her well-known allure. Occasionally she had thought she was breaking through the barrier, that she was getting somewhere with him, but then the barriers had come crashing down again, leaving her very firmly on the wrong side. She had wondered why every time he seemed to be thawing towards her it was as though something reminded him he wasn't supposed to like her.

Now she knew why. Well, that was all right with her. She had got the message. Friendly, but not too friendly. She didn't have time for a man in her life at the moment, not if she was really to make something of her career. And, furthermore, a man who was her boss would only complicate matters to an extent she couldn't bring herself to contemplate. OK, so there was a passing attraction. All right, maybe there was an element of infatuation about it. Adolescent, true, but that would be over soon. Infatuation never stood the test of seeing the hero's feet of clay and these she was seeing daily! All she had to do was stay out of his way and the whole thing would blow over.

Having finally resolved the situation to her own satisfaction, Jessica took herself off to bed, expecting to fall asleep with no problem. It only added to her confusion that she should pass a very restless night, her dreams punctuated with images of a very angry Mike.

Hughie sat facing her, but only his body was present; his mind was clearly somewhere else.

'How about a few days in hospital, Hughie?' she asked quietly, not really expecting a response.

'Nothing wrong with me,' came the grunted response.

'Yes, there is. You're becoming ill again, and we need to try to stop it before it gets worse.'

She was prepared for a long verbal battle with

Hughie, who usually strongly resisted any suggestion of hospitalisation. This time was no different. Rather than force the issue, Jessica suggested they review his medication and made a note that all staff needed to keep a careful watch on him. So long as he agreed to come to the day hospital all day, every day they might be able to help him maintain his shaky grip on sanity.

'Dr Balfour!' The peremptory tone stopped Jessica in her tracks and just for a second she had to think who would be calling her in that tone of voice. As she turned round, still uncertain, the female voice continued, 'We have to talk and get some things sorted out.'

Jeannie! If she hadn't seen it, or rather heard it with her own ears, Jessica wasn't sure that she would have believed it. The other woman was standing straighter than she habitually did and, as she closed in on Jessica, she could see that Jeannie even had a touch of lipstick on and her hair looked as though it had recently been styled. It was amazing what some responsibility and a real job could do for people's confidence and sense of self-worth. Jeannie was looking better than at any time Jessica could remember. Now she was waving a sheaf of papers in front of Jessica's astounded eyes, clearly determined on business.

'We really have to get all this sorted out, Doctor. You're holding everybody up at the moment.'

While Jessica was containing her astonishment and working on a way of handling the new-found confidence of her patient, she heard a deep chuckle behind her.

'That's it, Jeannie. Keep her hard at it! Someone round here has to get her to toe the line.' Mike's bass voice was warmly approving as Jessica, who hadn't heard him come up behind her, whirled round to confront him.

His face was split in a broad grin and Jessica felt her knees turn liquid as her eyes met and were held by his. As their gaze lengthened the laughter that had been in his faded, leaving a wariness in its place. What was in hers that should cause him to respond like that Jessica dreaded to think.

It seemed Jessica wasn't the only one to notice the abrupt change in Mike, but Jeannie, too, was attributing the change to her behaviour.

'S-sorry, Doctor...' she stammered. 'I know you're busy... I shouldn't have——'

Mike jumped in, interrupting the by now very anxious-looking woman. 'Don't you dare spoil it by apologising. You've got a major task on your hands, keeping the admin of this exhibition under control, and you're doing a splendid job of it. It also means trying to keep some control on Dr Balfour—no easy task, as I know to my cost. You keep her in line over this and the rest of us will be eternally grateful.' And, bestowing one of his megawatt smiles on the now blushing woman, he left them staring after him in the corridor.

'Isn't he wonderful?' Jeannie breathed, clearly smitten by Mike's undoubted charm.

'Oh, yes, wonderful,' Jessica agreed with such a wealth of sarcasm in her tone that Jeannie gave the younger doctor a very speculative look before once again waving the papers at her. Jessica gave in with good grace, realising that she had to keep a greater control over her emotions about Mike when she was talking to patients. Not only couldn't she afford any hint of speculation, it was also most unprofessional, not to say unfair to Mike, to hint at anything untoward between them.

Not that there *was* anything between them. Maybe that was the trouble. It was a couple of weeks since she had decided seeing less of Mike would be sensible. She had stuck closely to her plan of avoiding him as much as she could and had been surprised by how little they really needed to see of each other. Despite their offices being next door to one another, they rarely exchanged more than a hello in the corridor. Of course they had to meet to discuss patients and the running of the day hospital, and they met in the usual staff and business meetings, but that was all. They managed to take their coffee at different times in the staffroom or, increasingly, both of them kept to their own rooms for coffee. When they did meet they never exchanged more than a few words, nothing remotely personal entered into their conversation.

At first Jessica had been immensely relieved, but as one week became two, then three, approaching four, she began to suspect that Mike was also trying to keep out of her way. For all its resources, in a building as small as the day hospital it would take two to avoid each other so completely. As she realised this a slow resentment began to burn in Jessica. Just who did Michael Knight think he was? So the name Michael meant like God—she felt a twinge of embarassment as she remembered looking it up—and, true, he resembled nothing so much as a god-like figure from Norse mythology, not counting the fact that he was the sexiest thing on two legs she had ever encountered, but that he should feel the need to avoid her. . .! What did he think she was going to do? Fall on him in a frenzy of unbridled lust?

Her cheeks flamed as she accepted that, of course, that was exactly what she wanted to do! A small cough beside her brought her back to the cold reality of the present and the still speculative glance of Jeannie MacPherson. She gave in to the inevitable.

'Would now be a good time?'

Jeannie had surpassed all expectations in her handling of the work for the exhibition, even prompting Mike to acknowledge that it had been 'a good idea' of Jessica's. The protected environment of the hospital gave Jeannie the confidence to take things at her own pace and stop work when she felt herself getting overwhelmed. Her obsessive tendencies had, as Jessica had predicted, come into their own as she checked everything several times over, and never once had there been a mistake. Jessica was working with her to try to cut down on some of the checking, but was pleased to note that some of Jeannie's other obsessive rituals seemed to have disappeared of their own accord. Jeannie herself had made a self-deprecating comment about it at one point, saying she didn't have time for them, now she had more interesting things to do. Her depression had lifted to a great extent, but the underlying problems of low self-esteem and lack of self-worth were still there and needed dealing with. Up until this moment Jessica would have said assertiveness was also a problem, but now she wasn't so sure. Maybe Jeannie had the right skills but had just forgotten how to use them.

'I've answered all the straightforward ones, sending out application forms,' Jeannie announced. She pushed forward a small box of record cards. 'These are details of the people who've said they are sending stuff in, with a note of whether they've paid their hanging fee or not. All the money has gone to Mr Smith.' She glanced down at the list in her hand as she ticked the items off. 'So far we've got over one hundred and fifty entries from all over Britain and they're still coming in.'

'How many?' Jessica's voice was an inelegant squawk and Jeannie gave a small, self-satisfied smile as she got the response she had been hoping for.

'One hundred and fifty,' she repeated obediently. 'And more coming in every day.'

'Where on earth are we going to put them all?' For the first time since she had dreamed up her 'good idea', Jessica fully realised the enormity of what she had taken on. At the beginning, despite her contempt at the suggestion that it was nothing more than pinning up a few pictures, she hadn't really understood just how much work was involved and how many people it would encompass. Nor just how important it would be to them. Some of the letters they had had were full of enthusiasm for the idea, and some of them had moved her close to tears. Harry Smith, the accountant, was not the only person who had gone back to a discarded hobby. Several people had written to say they had stopped painting when they became ill, but this exhibition had prompted them to start again. They were effusive in their thanks and Jessica felt guilty over the little thought she had put into the consequences of her plan.

There had also been some surprise at the number of trained, professional artists who had responded to the advertisement in the artists' magazine who had suffered from psychological problems at one time or another. A couple referred to their episodes of mania, which caused Jessica to recall that some work had been done linking manic-depression—or bipolar affective disorder as it was now usually called—with creativity. Stuart had gone off and looked the research up and presented it at the registrar's journal club, while Naomi was writing a review article for an occupational therapy journal. Far-reaching consequences, indeed.

'There's loads of space when you work it out,' Jeannie answered seriously, although Jessica knew that her question had been largely rhetorical. 'But just at the moment I need to know what you want doing with these.' And once again she waved the pile of letters at Jessica.

'Tell me,' she sighed, knowing that she had been putting off dealing with some of the letters she would have to answer personally.

'Well, there's a suggestion from two social workers who write their own songs that they could come and perform, and also one from a group of community psychiatric nurses who want to put on a mime show. Then there's a woman who wants to know how high our ceilings are for her kinetic sculptures, and a man who wants to know about fire regulations and our electricity supply as his work involves—and I'm quoting him now—"demonstrating my contempt for the way society pushes people with mental illness to the fringes by shorting out the power-point and incorporating the fire into a dynamic work of art".'

'You're making this up!'

'I am not!' Jeannie sounded most indignant at the idea. 'There's just a lot of funny people in the world,' she pronounced, straight-faced. 'Personally, I like the idea of miming nurses, but I suppose. . .' Her voice trailed off.

'You suppose right,' Jessica affirmed quickly. 'No to

them all. We haven't got the space,' she explained, sensing the other woman's disappointment.

Jeannie grinned, leading Jessica to wonder just how far she was being teased, then added, 'If you can write the letters today, I'll get them typed and sent off tomorrow.'

'Right. Leave them with me.' Jessica knew when she was beaten and gave in with good grace.

At the door Jeannie twisted back to Jessica, her manner now more diffident. 'I hope it's all right, but Rose is giving me a hand with some of this.'

'Rose?' Jessica frowned, trying to place the name.

'A new patient. One of Dr James's. Took an overdose.'

'Oh, yes.' Jessica remembered the new woman who was coming into the day hospital a couple of days a week. A slightly overweight middle-aged woman who couldn't look anyone in the eye. Being with Jeannie would probably do her the world of good.

'Thought it would give her something else to think about,' Jeannie muttered, and hurried out.

She was quickly replaced by Shona Whyte, whose pregnancy was progressing well, as was her fight against the depression that so frequently overwhelmed her. So far, so good, they had told each other. Archie Duff had proved to be a gem of an obstetrician and had supported Shona throughout the pregnancy with a skill and compassion that had impressed Jessica enormously. And now they only had a week to go.

'You're looking well.' Jessica sank thankfully down in a comfy armchair in Val's living-room and eased her feet out of her shoes, glad that this time she could utter the words and know them to be true. Val was now seven months pregnant and blooming, although, after her earlier scare, was sensibly taking things easily.

'That's more than I can say for you,' the older woman responded candidly. 'What's the matter? You're looking...washed out, somehow. Are you working too hard or something?'

Shaking her head, Jessica sought a reply that would satisfy her friend without giving anything away of her inner turmoil. Secretly she was horrified that Val had noticed any difference in her appearance and wondered if it was seen by others. She had thought that she was maintaining a perfectly normal face to the world. 'Just a bit tired, that's all. The exhibition is taking more time than I expected and——'

'Yes, tell me about it,' Val butted in. 'Mike was saying that——'

'Mike?' As she spoke Jessica knew that her tone was sharper than was warranted and knew, too, that Val would pick up on it. In that she wasn't disappointed.

'Like that, is it?' she asked with a knowing grin. 'I thought he was a bit strained when I mentioned you.'

'Like what?' Jessica demanded with a touch of belligerence. 'There's nothing between Michael Knight and me and——'

'That's what he said, too,' Val confirmed with a wide grin. 'So how come I don't believe it?'

With an unexpectedness which surprised her all the fight suddenly went out of Jessica and her dark eyes clouded over as they filled with unwanted tears.

'Jessie...! What on earth...?' Val sounded more shocked than Jessica felt. 'I think you had better tell me what's going on.'

Even while she was shaking her head and getting ready to deny everything Jessica was overtaken by a sense of wanting to share her confused thoughts and feelings with someone else. Not absolutely everything, of course, but a second opinion about Mike's behaviour would be welcome. So, with a sniff and a lot of rapid blinking of her eyes to disperse the tears, she poured out an only slightly edited version of the story starting with Mike rescuing her in the snow, then in the hotel, and ending with his falling down the stairs. She stuttered to a halt then, remembering how that had ended in his office with him kissing her, and she had a sense of loss as she wondered if that was going to be the only time.

'And the rest.' Val's voice cut across her thoughts.

'What?'

'Whatever caused you to stop like that and look so bereft,' Val elaborated.

Cheeks flaming, Jessica told her about Mike kissing her and her conviction that now he was avoiding her. At the end of her story she was totally confounded by Val's laughing and saying, 'Poor Mike. No wonder he sounded strained.'

'What do you mean "poor Mike"? What about me? I'm the one who doesn't know whether I'm coming or going.'

'Yes, I can see that,' Val confirmed. 'One step forward and two back sort of thing.'

'It's more a step forward and then he shoots off at a tangent,' Jessica elaborated, thinking about his recent behaviour. 'What are you grinning about now?' For Val's face had split in a wide grin of pure amusement.

'Your description of Mike's behaviour. Knight's move.' And added, at Jessica's blank look, 'You know, as in chess.'

'Yes, very clever, but what about some advice?'

'I don't think I've got any to give. He doesn't like helpless women and that's how he has cast you. After all, what have you done but get into scrapes since you've met him? And he's got you out of them.'

Sunk in gloom, Jessica felt that Val could have sounded more sympathetic. In fact she sounded suspiciously cheerful about it.

'If it's any consolation to you, though,' Val added, drawing out her words slowly, forcing Jessica to look up and pay attention, 'I think he's having serious trouble ignoring you. My instincts tell me that, despite his best intentions, you've got under his skin and he's fighting off his attraction to you.'

Jessica wasn't totally convinced, but Val kept pressing home her point and by the time she left she was feeling more positive than she had been and certainly had a lot to think about.

Graham caught up with her as she hurried down the corridor, grabbing her by the arm to halt her progress before unceremoniously pulling her into the staffroom.

'What on earth. . .?' Jessica began indignantly, wresting her arm from Graham's grip, her anger at being so manhandled dissipating somewhat as she took in Graham's worried face and his apparently total lack of awareness of what he had just done.

'It's Hughie,' he informed her, catching his breath. 'I've just had the police on the phone and——'

'The police!' Jessica's anger vanished. She was prepared to be hustled in the patients' interests and if there was nothing personal in it.

'They're at Hughie's flat. Apparently he was out early this morning hurling abuse at the neighbours and has now barricaded himself in.'

'Why don't they leave him alone? He'll come out sooner or later. Usually sooner. He's done it before.'

'Yes, but one of the neighbours called the police and they seem to think something should be done.'

'We'd better go down.' Jessica gave a resigned sigh as she glanced at the window. Why did these things always happen when it was pouring with rain?

'Yes. The police were muttering something about breaking the door down.'

'For goodness' sake! Why?' Jessica was struggling into her raincoat and now took in, for the first time, that Graham was already dressed in his coat. So much for her making the decisions!

'Maybe it's a quiet day,' Graham responded, without so much as a flicker of amusement crossing his face. But Jessica caught the twinkle in his eyes.

Graham was patiently talking to Hughie through the letterbox, and had managed to establish some sort of conversation with him, but Hughie was adamant. He wasn't coming out and no one was coming in.

Jessica pushed her wet hair back from her face. Despite the covered walkway that ran the length of the flats, the wind was blowing the rain underneath and they were all wet. At least it meant that the nosy neighbours had got fed up and gone off. Now all that was left was her, Graham and two increasingly bored young policemen. Jessica had tried to persuade them to leave, but they were determined to stay. She had the sinking feeling that they were still hoping to break down the door.

'Let me have another go.' She took Graham's place and crouched before the door. 'Hughie. It's me. Dr

Balfour. Will you let me in? Just me. I want to talk to you.'

Hughie's, 'Go away,' came surrounded by more colourful language, but Jessica was undaunted.

'Please, Hughie. We need to talk and sort this mess out.'

'Talk to them next door. They're the ones trying to kill me.' Hughie was explicit in what he would do to them if he did come out.

Jessica straightened and turned back to the three men, just in time to get a face full of rain as a particularly strong gust of wind blew it across the walkway. Cold, tired, fed up and very wet, Jessica had had enough. Pivoting back to the front door, she thumped on it with a force which made all three men take a step back.

'Hughie, open this damned door and let me in! I'm cold, soaked to the skin and I've had all I'm going to take from you, so you'd——' She didn't have time to finish the sentence. The door opened and Hughie stood there, glaring.

'Why didn't you say so?' he muttered, standing back to let Jessica in. 'Only her,' he growled, squaring up to the two policemen when they would have shouldered their way past him.

'It's all right,' Jessica assured them. 'You wait here.'

'I'll come too.' Graham faced Hughie straight on, daring him to refuse him entry. His macho stance was only slightly spoilt by the rain dripping from his hair and running off the end of his nose, making him look more like a wee boy due for a scolding from his mother for playing in the rain than a Glasgow hard man, but something in his stance satisfied Hughie for, with not so much as a murmur, he stood back and let Graham enter before closing the door quickly and firmly in the face of the police.

Now that they had got into the house Hughie seemed to calm down, as though having them there aided his control. A quick glance round told Jessica that there was nothing out of the ordinary except for a couple of chairs pushed up by the front door. So much for a 'barricade'!

'This has all got a bit out of hand, hasn't it?' she asked Hughie conversationally and was pleased when he nodded.

'Aye.' She waited to see if he would say anything else, and later owned to being surprised when he added, 'I expect you'll want to admit me.'

'I think it's best, don't you?' She tried to smile, but saw the blank despair in Hughie's face and knew that such simple reassurance was not only inappropriate but insulting. 'It shouldn't be for too long. We can sort out your medication and it'll give the neighbours time to calm down.'

'Aye.' The defeat was palpable and Jessica somehow felt she had failed him. But there was nothing else to do. 'Do your worst, Doctor.'

'Graham will help you get your things together and we'll drive you there. No need for an ambulance.'

'Thanks, Doctor.' Hughie tried a smile, but it was nothing more than a twisting of his lip.

The two men went into the bedroom and Jessica went out to tell the police, who were clearly relieved at the peaceful outcome but nevertheless insisted on escorting Jessica and her charge to St Mungo's.

'I think she was all set to start hurling abuse back at him.' Graham was recounting the incident to the rest

KNIGHT'S MOVE 95

of the staff over coffee the next morning, making Jessica's actions sound much more dramatic than she thought was warranted. She was conscious of Mike's speculative gaze on her, but refused to meet his eye. Overnight she had come to some decisions about a new approach to Hughie's medication, but would need to talk to Mike. She would leave him a note.

CHAPTER SIX

'MAYBE you could use this space to put the sculptures you're going to get. . .' The small, dark woman darted around the open-plan dining area, an expression of fierce concentration on her face. Alison McNaughton owned a local art gallery and Jessica had enlisted her help for the exhibition. Or, rather, was picking her brains for suggestions. Ms McNaughton, as she wanted to be called, didn't have too much time to give for actual 'help'. By now Jessica wasn't at all sure she had done the right thing. The space was all wrong, the dimensions of the corridors a problem, the lighting appalling. . . Ms McNaughton's list of complaints about the building's suitability for an exhibition was never-ending. Jessica didn't know which she regretted more—the idea of the exhibition or inviting Alison McNaughton along for advice.

Yes, she did, and it was definitely the latter. Out of the corner of her eye, she saw Mike bearing down on them, a gleam in his navy blue eyes as they alighted on the trim figure of the petite Alison in figure-hugging red. Next to her five feet Jessica felt like a giantess, and even the sight of Mike stooping at the waist to introduce himself to the other woman didn't make her feel any better. So Alison looked like a doll next to him. It seemed that Mike would be very happy to pick the doll up in one hand and make off with her. Why was it that tall men always seemed to be attracted to short women? It wasn't fair. Neither of these thoughts did anything to improve Jessica's mood.

'Cheer up, Doctor. It can't be that bad.' She hadn't heard Maggie come up to join her. She looked worried for a second. 'Can it?'

Hastily Jessica sought to reassure her. 'No, no. I was just thinking about the exhibition—where everything's going to go, that sort of thing.'

The look of relief on Maggie's face was evident and that told Jessica its own story. 'You've nothing to worry about there, then. It's a grand idea. It'll all look great. You wait and see.' Then, lighting a fresh cigarette from the stub of the one she was finishing, she wandered away, muttering 'Grand, just grand,' under her breath.

'Jessica, can you come and speak to Mr Morris?' Now it was Graham who had appeared silently. 'I can't get him to tell me what the problem is with his wife. He's on the phone and insisting on talking to a doctor.'

As she left the dining-room she couldn't help but let her eyes drift back to where Mike and Alison were deep in conversation as they regarded the long, blank wall where she planned to hang some of the best pictures. The top of Alison's head reached halfway up Mike's chest. Something about the sight made her want to cry.

'Jessica, I want a word with you.' The tone matched the words, and both sounded ominous to a bewildered Jessica, but she had no choice but to precede Mike into his room.

Since her conversation with Val she had veered violently between wanting to believe what Val had said about Mike being attracted to her but fighting against it, and believing it was nothing more than wishful thinking. Too confused even to think clearly, she was keeping out of his way more than ever, leaving him notes and memos rather than speaking directly to him whenever possible. He had said nothing for several days and she thought that she had got away with it and that he was as happy as she to reduce their contact to a minimum. Now this summons.

'Have a seat.' Mike walked round his desk and took a seat opposite her. The wide expanse of polished wood between them seemed as wide and as barren as a desert to Jessica and only emphasised how little they related to each other. The formality of the situation was unmistakable. He didn't say anything but spent several seconds simply watching her, his eyes travelling slowly, assessingly over her but not meeting hers. There was nothing sexual in the gaze; it was more as though he were observing some interesting new scientific specimen. Just as Jessica was wondering if he was testing her in some way, waiting to see how long it would take her before she spoke, he broke the silence himself.

'This can't go on, you know.' His voice was even, controlled, but Jessica sensed that it was something of an effort for him to sound so disinterested. Immediately she guessed that he was referring to the notes she was leaving for him, but couldn't bring herself to admit that. If he wanted to bring everything out into the open that was up to him, but he would have to do it alone—she wasn't going to help any more than she had to.

As it became obvious that Jessica wasn't going to say anything Mike's expression changed from cool control and he let some of his real feelings show. Feelings that appeared to be closer to anger than anything else. That in itself surprised Jessica. Irritation would have been closer to the mark, she would have supposed, but the frown that was creasing Mike's brow was several degrees beyond irritation.

Realising that he would have to spell it out to her, Mike pushed several of her notes across his desk to her. 'I realise we haven't always seen eye to eye in the past, but don't you think this is going a bit too far? We have to communicate—about patients, about the day hospital, at the very least. Writing notes simply isn't enough.'

Jessica shrugged, keeping her eyes glued on her clasped hands resting in her lap, knowing that the gesture bordered on the insolent and that Mike would very likely take it that way but finding it difficult to know what to say. She couldn't deny what he said, but neither could she explain. With hindsight, she accepted that she had gone too far and that she could have kept out of Mike's way much more subtly. She needn't have gone overboard like this. Briefly it crossed her mind that she might have done it deliberately, to make Mike acknowledge the situation between them. If she had, then she had certainly got her wish now.

She heard Mike take a deep breath before he demanded, 'Jessica, at least look at me when I'm talking to you.' At this, she knew she had no choice and lifted her eyes to meet his gaze, but only for an instant as she broke the contact, focusing her eyes on the knot of his silk tie. 'We have to find a way of working this out. I realise that you don't want to work with me, but I also assume that you don't want to leave your job.'

Leave her job? What was he talking about? Jessica sat up straighter and paid attention. Things were rapidly getting out of hand. Change jobs? No way. And no way did she want anyone else to know of the problems they were having. The last thing she needed was to be branded difficult or hard to get along with. That would put paid to all her career plans. She had to set about doing something to retrieve the situation.

'No, of course, I don't want to leave this job.'

Now that she had finally spoken some of the tension seemed to go out of Mike and he leant back in his chair for a moment, eyes warily fixed on her, before suddenly leaning forward again to challenge her across the desk. 'Well, what are you going to do, then?'

'Er. . .do I have to do anything?' she asked, sounding more of a helpless female than she had intended. 'I mean, we can talk about. . .about the things that we have to talk about and. . .er. . .' She trailed off. There should be something else but, just at the moment, with Mike's violet-blue eyes holding her own against her will, she couldn't think what it was.

'And the fact that you've been avoiding me to the point that even the patients have noticed and are talking about it?'

She was genuinely surprised at that. And worried. Whatever her problems in dealing with Mike she had never intended them to affect anyone else, the patients least of all. 'Are you sure?'

'Yes.' His uncompromising tone dared her to challenge his assertion and, after all, why would he lie about it?

'I haven't been deliberately avoiding you.' She offered the blatant lie as a way out, but it seemed that Mike wasn't going to settle for half-measures as his eyebrow rocketed sky-high although he refrained from commenting.

'Well, no more than you've been avoiding me,' she said, accepting his challenge and offering one of her own, meeting his eyes squarely in open provocation. She then proceeded to watch in delighted fascination as the colour ran up under his skin, the tide of crimson washing his cheekbones—but Jessica had to admire the fact that, despite his obvious embarrassment, he didn't break their eye contact. It was left to her to blink and reduce the tension that was mounting.

'You're right, of course,' he admitted in a husky voice that sent shivers through Jessica, although whether it was his tone or what he said that caused the reaction she couldn't have said. The last thing she had expected was that he would admit that he had been avoiding her. Her heart sank, but she forced herself to pay attention to what he was saying. 'I thought a bit of distance between us would convince you that I meant what I said, but it only seemed to make matters worse. I thought you had accepted that it was an aberration on my part and that we could forget it.'

Jessica felt like Alice when she had wandered through the looking-glass. She understood the words—she even understood the sentences—but for the life of her she couldn't make sense of what he was saying. Mike got up from his desk and wandered over to the window, his back to her, looking out across the car park as though the view were so fascinating, he couldn't tear his gaze away.

'If you can't forget it, can you at least accept——?'

'Mike, I have to say that I don't know what you're talking about!'

The admission brought him spinning round to face her, his expression comically dismayed. 'But. . . I thought that. . .' He stopped, took a deep breath and tried again. 'Maybe we had better start at the beginning and you tell me why you have been avoiding me.' This was the consultant psychiatrist back in control again and that didn't help Jessica. She knew she didn't have an acceptable answer to give him and the truth was out of the question. That left taking the challenge back into his court.

'Maybe it would be better to clear up this misunderstanding first,' she countered, and knew that she had scored points when Mike turned away from her back to his contemplation of the car park.

'I kissed you,' he supplied simply. 'I thought this was your way of telling me that my behaviour was out of line, or that you thought I would expect to do it again. Maybe, even, that you thought it was harassment. I believed you when you accepted my apology at the time, but then wondered if it made you feel vulnerable working with me. I thought giving you a bit of space would indicate that it was, as I said, an aberration and not something I habitually deal in with younger female colleagues.'

Drawing a deep breath, Jessica felt her heart lift. First of all, Mike's concern about his behaviour showed that he was basically a decent man and she should never have doubted it and, secondly, she saw it as giving her a way out.

'I think there's been a bit of confusion here,' she began slowly as she tried to grapple with the intricacies of the story she was about to weave. Yes, it would work. It was so simple. 'True, I might have avoided you a bit after that night, but it was because I was embarrassed. After all, it *was* my fault you fell downstairs—'

'*Now* she admits it,' Mike muttered, but Jessica ignored him.

'—and I did believe you about the kiss—I mean about it being a mistake and something we should forget about.' If only I could, passed through her mind, but she kept speaking. 'And then it seemed to me that you were avoiding me, so I thought I'd make it easy by avoiding you and. . .well. . .it all seems to have got a trifle out of hand.' She managed a very creditable smile which mixed apology with amusement, embarrassment with a no-real-damage-done kind of confidence.

'Hmm.' The look Mike was giving her indicated that although her story was plausible he didn't altogether believe her but that he had the sense not to challenge her on it. 'OK. If you say so.' He shrugged and returned to his desk, pushing some papers into his briefcase. Taking the gesture as one of dismissal, Jessica hurried to the door. But she wasn't safe yet. Not quite.

'If, as you say, it was all a misunderstanding, maybe we should have a drink together and settle the matter once and for all.'

'Er. . .if you think that's necessary.'

'Yes, I do. I'll pick you up about seven-thirty. Now I'm off to St Mungo's for the rest of the day.' He gave as his destination the local psychiatric hospital into whose catchment area they fell.

Her emotions see-sawing, Jessica could only nod blankly at him. 'Yes. You'll want my address. It's——'

'Got it.' Mike winked at her and was gone.

Jessica could hear him running down the stairs as she drew together the tattered shreds of her composure. At least she was going to see him, and maybe she could even turn this into the start of a new relationship between them.

It seemed the most natural thing in the world to move to the window to watch Mike cross the car park and get into his car. A squeal of brakes and skidding tyres drew her attention and she watched, horrified, as an out-of-control car swerved crazily across the road and into the car park before executing a messy three-point turn and heading back the way it had come. Even from this distance she could see that it was driven by children. The stealing and driving of cars by young boys was a growing problem in the area. She phoned down to Janet at Reception to ask her to notify the police with details of the car and the general direction they were headed without any real hope that it would do any good and, sighing, headed back to her own room. The instant she stepped into the corridor she was immediately greeted by a harassed Naomi.

'There you are! Could you come and have a word with Rose? I don't know what Stuart has been saying to her but she's very upset, and I can't get her calmed down.'

Rose was indeed upset and in an agitated state when Jessica reached her, but gradually she pieced together what had happened. Rose had suffered from depression on and off for some time and a few weeks ago had taken an overdose. Not a very big one, but it could have been fatal. Her husband had found her and she had been rushed to the hospital where her stomach had been pumped. She was making a slow recovery, embarassment about what she had done adding to her other problems. Now it seemed that Stuart had told her that it was all due to the menopause and that she was behaving like a 'typical hysterical woman'.

Jessica didn't want to believe that Stuart had said something so stupid and potentially harmful—particularly when none of it was true. Unfortunately, her imagination supplied the scenario only too well. Stuart found it hard to relate to middle-aged female patients and Jessica could just bring herself to believe that, frustrated and unable to deal with the situation, he might possibly say something so inappropriate.

Rose was eventually calmed down enough to go off for a restoring cup of tea and Jessica went in search of Stuart, finding him in the staff room. At first he denied saying anything, but eventually admitted it.

'What's the harm? These middle-aged women are all the same. I pity her poor husband. He's the one who——'

Jessica couldn't take any more of the young man's arrogance and launched into the attack. They were still hurling abuse at one another when Naomi rushed in, slamming the door behind her.

'What the hell do you two think you're playing at? You can be heard all over the hospital! You should both have more sense. God alone knows what the patients must be thinking.'

Jessica was immediately contrite but Stuart was still inclined to be difficult, shrugging and muttering under his breath.

'Oh, grow up and stop behaving like a wee boy.' Naomi had no time to be tactful.

Turning very pink about the ears, Stuart gabbled a few words about them not hearing the last of this before he walked with injured dignity from the room.

'Give me strength!' Jessica sank down into an armchair, cupping her face in her hands as she massaged her temples. 'Could you really. . .?' She couldn't bring herself to ask the rest of the question, but Naomi knew what she meant.

'It wasn't quite that bad, but you could be heard in the corridor. What on earth possessed you?'

'I guess I've had just about enough of Stuart and his patronising, "little woman" bit. And someone had to tell him that he can't go round saying things like that to a patient.'

'And you just decided to be tactful about it?' Naomi commented on a grin. 'Come on, let's have a coffee and get back to normal.'

'Right. I don't know why they let men become psychiatrists in the first place,' Jessica grumbled. 'They're all totally insensitive and——' She caught sight of Naomi's astonished face. 'All right, all right, I'm just having a bad day. Don't take any notice of me.'

And then the day improved. Barry, Shona's husband, rang to say that Shona had just had a baby boy. Dropping everything, Jessica rushed off to see her patient and the new infant. Tired but exultant, Shona showed her baby off and, gently cradling the tiny, very pink bundle, Jessica was overwhelmed with a feeling of joy. Between them, they had got Shona through this pregnancy without any major upsets in her mental health. It was an achievement of which they could all be justifiably proud. And now this. A new life cradled in her arms. Even as part of her mind ran on the continuing care and support Shona would need another part—a part she hadn't known she had—surfaced as a wave of maternal emotion flooded out all other sensation. At that moment Jessica was aware of a desire to be holding a child of her own. A baby she had created with a man she loved. But she had no one.

With tears in her eyes Jessica handed the infant back to his proud mother and firmly repressed the maternal feelings she hadn't known she possessed. What, after all, could she do about them?

At half-past six the phone rang.

'Have you eaten yet?' No hello, no introduction, but Jessica knew she would recognise those deep velvet tones anywhere.

'No.' She thought of the omelette turning to rubber on the stove even as she spoke.

'Well, don't. I'll be late and won't have eaten, so we'll grab a bite somewhere. I'll get to you around eight-fifteen.' He rang off before she could even utter a word of agreement.

As she tipped the inedible mass of overcooked eggs into the bin two hours seemed a long time to wait for food. Reaching for an apple, Jessica hoped it would stave off the hunger pangs.

The extra time gave her longer to worry about how to behave—what to say, what to wear. It could hardly be classed as a date but she didn't want to wear her work suit and, after the times Mike had seen her looking a mess, she felt a very special need to look presentable. Admit it, she insisted to herself, you mean attractive.

She looked at herself in the long mirror in her bedroom. Maybe the trousers she was wearing were too casual if they were going to eat out, although he hadn't made it sound as though they were going anywhere elaborate. She changed into a soft silk dress. No, that looked as though she was trying too hard. She tried a favourite full skirt and decided it made her look dumpy. She remembered Mike's eyes roving over

Geena's Lycra-clad curves at the hairdressers; the full skirt came off.

By eight o'clock she was in a panic. Everything she owned was either unflattering, out of date, too formal or too casual. Nothing seemed remotely possible. Why do I care? she asked herself. The man, for all that he's the sexiest thing I've ever seen, is my boss. That's all there is to it. And this is just a meeting about work—informal, yes, but nothing to get worked up about. Maybe the trousers were the answer after all.

She pulled the slim-fitting black trousers back on and added a figure-skimming coral jumper, not noticing how the colour lifted her skin tone and made her dark brown hair glow with fiery highlights, nor how the length of her legs was emphasised as her shape was delicately hinted at. Big gold earrings and a wide gold cuff stopped the outfit appearing too casual without making it inappropriate for a local pub or small restaurant—wherever they ended up. She was retouching her lipstick—a coral shade darker than her jumper—when her entry phone rang and she went to let Mike in.

She was proud of her flat and the way she had redecorated. Not that it was finished yet, by any means, but she knew the coral and cream of the hall, set off by touches of black and gold, were a perfect foil for her and so she was somewhat disappointed when Mike didn't even glance round him when she invited him in, but merely instructed her to get her coat.

'Hurry up, I'm starving.' He was still in the suit he had been wearing that morning, a jacket slung over that, and Jessica guessed he hadn't even found the time for an apple! It didn't take much to appreciate that keeping his massive frame fuelled would take regular meals but she couldn't quite suppress a sense of disappointment as she followed him out to his car. She had never asked him what had happened to the Range Rover he had been driving the first time they met and now didn't seem the right time either. It would probably remain one of those little mysteries to which she would never learn the answer.

The wine bar wasn't quite what Jessica had expected—noisy and crowded—but the small restaurant at its back proved to be an unexpected bonus—quiet, relaxed but not overly intimate, and with a small but interesting menu. Mike absently picked up a piece of bread as he looked at the menu and Jessica couldn't help smiling to herself. Noticing the smile, Mike matched it before realising what had caused her amusement. He looked slightly embarrassed, putting the bread down and pointedly offering the basket to her, which she declined on principle, although it did look remarkably good. What the principle was she couldn't have articulated at that moment, but it seemed some kind of statement.

'Sorry.' Mike looked longingly at the bread and Jessica was forcibly reminded of a small boy who had been reprimanded for bad manners and told to wait before starting.

Nodding at the bread and grinning, Jessica told him, 'Don't mind me. Carry on.'

The endearingly sheepish grin he gave went straight to Jessica's heart, sending her pulse sky-high. 'Thanks. All I got for lunch was an apple.'

'No wonder you said you were starving.'

'Mmm.' He finished the bread and grinned again. 'That's better. I wouldn't have wanted to keel over with hunger!'

'No, there's rather too much of you to pick up easily.' For a moment Jessica wondered if she had presumed too far on their tenuous relationship as something she couldn't identify flickered in his eyes, but then he was smiling at her again and whatever she thought she had seen vanished and they became merely amused, fine lines fanning out from their corners. Her fingers itched to smooth them away, to stroke the firm lines of his chin. Resolutely she gripped her hands together under the table.

She had thought they were going to talk about the running of the hospital, about the exhibition, about anything to do with work, but not about their favourite Shakespeare plays, the relative merits of Pavarotti and Placido Domingo, about poetry and their memories of singing in the school choir. She couldn't remember the last time she had had such an interesting conversation with a man—a man who, furthermore, had tastes so similar to her own.

The wine was releasing her tensions, lowering her inhibitions, and she found herself mesmerised by his deep, bass voice as her eyes focused on the sensual lips from which the sounds were issuing, watching their movement as they shaped words, watching as the lips pursed and stretched round vowels and consonants. They looked soft but strong, warm, dry, beautifully shaped. They looked as though they belonged on a work of art. They were art. She wanted to reach out and touch them.

She had touched them! Her memory flew back to the one time Mike had kissed her. It wasn't enough, not nearly enough. She wanted to be able to run her fingers along his jawline, then back to stroke his lips. She wanted him to kiss her again, to feel him smoothing the skin of her neck, her shoulders as his lips moved down and down, trailing a path to——

'Jessica, are you all right?' Mike's voice intruded into her thoughts just at the point when she realised exactly what she was thinking, about whom, and in the middle of a public restaurant. Cheeks scarlet, she took a hasty gulp of wine and then nearly choked as she had trouble swallowing.

'Fine,' she gasped, eyes watering, but at least she now had a reason for her heightened colour and confusion.

'Are you sure? You looked miles away.' His head was tilted to one side and Jessica wasn't altogether sure she liked the assessing look which was back in Mike's eyes.

'Yes, really.' She risked another quick glance at Mike's face but, unable to meet his eyes without blushing again, rapidly looked away. Her glance had told her that a smile was tugging at the corners of his mouth and he was looking peculiarly smug.

'I'm not so bad once you get to know me, am I?' he astounded her by saying. 'Until you went off into your daydream I thought we were getting along very nicely. I hope it wasn't anything I said.'

Since he couldn't possibly know what she had been thinking, why was he looking so pleased with himself? Jessica had a sense of somehow having lost control of the situation, of not being sure where she was being led, but nevertheless also sensed that Mike knew exactly what he was doing.

It apparently didn't surprise him that she said nothing and he continued to astonish Jessica further. 'I think it's clear that most of the "misunderstanding"—as you like to call it—between us stems from the fact that we're attracted to each other but that in the circumstances it's difficult to do anything about it. However, I think we're both adult enough, and well thought of enough by others to handle the consequences. And it isn't as though I'm going to be your boss for all that much longer. So I don't see that there is a problem.'

'Problem?'

'With our having an affair.'

CHAPTER SEVEN

'DOCTOR, where do you want this put?'

'There are two more downstairs; shall we bring them up?'

'See here, Doctor, you're going to have to shift your desk out of the way.'

Jessica felt like screaming. Never in her wildest nightmares had arranging an exhibition been like this. Her office was so crammed with paintings, photographs, sculptures, pottery and various things that defied labelling that there was barely room to move. With two weeks to go to the exhibition Jessica regretted, fervently and whole-heartedly, ever believing she had had 'a good idea'. It was an awful idea. The worst possible idea that anyone could ever have had. The fact that everyone else was excited and enthusiastic only seemed to make her despondency worse. Of course she covered it up as best she could, but knew that she wasn't always as successful as she would have liked. Most people didn't seem to notice her lack of enthusiasm and the problems she had in dragging through the days, but she had once noticed Naomi giving her a very penetrating look. Fortunately all she had said was a quiet, 'Is everything OK?' and, getting an affirmative answer, had left it at nothing more than, 'If you want to talk at any time. . .' Jessica had smiled her appreciation of the older woman's understanding but had said nothing more.

Three months had passed since her dinner with Mike

Knight and Jessica couldn't remember a worse, more unhappy three months. Shock had held her silent for long seconds after Mike's incredible proposition and he had taken that as assent that he should continue. He had outlined cold-bloodedly how an affair would suit them both; how she had made it clear that she didn't want marriage or a relationship that would interfere with her career; how, since he wasn't looking to get married either, this arrangement would be ideal—could even prove to be mutually beneficial in professional terms—until he had realised that Jessica's silence wasn't acquiescence but horror, was not approval of his plan but outright rejection.

What shamed Jessica was that she knew in her heart that if he hadn't been quite so cold-blooded about it, if he had offered her one word of warmth or affection, she would have agreed to anything he suggested. But something that was nothing more than a convenient arrangement. . . No, that she couldn't live with. It had hurt that Mike had seemed so surprised by her refusal, then had turned painfully sarcastic as he'd accused her of being like all women, saying one thing but meaning another. 'You might profess to be wedded to your career,' he had told her unforgivingly, 'but underneath it all all you want is a man to marry you and look after you. Well, I'm not offering that—ever.'

Both of them had then said things that would have been better left unsaid, but it was too late for recriminations. Jessica had left the restaurant and found a taxi to take her home rather than have to spend more time with Mike, and he had pointedly walked off in the opposite direction. Since then they had acted as though that awful evening had never happened. They were unfailingly polite to each other, dealt with matters pertaining to the management of both the day hospital and patients calmly and competently, and never exchanged one unnecessary word, one smile, one personal exchange of any kind.

That wasn't quite true. There had been one occasion, when the news had come through that Val had been safely delivered of a baby girl. John, Val's husband, had brought several bottles of champagne down to the day hospital for them to wet the baby's head and they had enjoyed a toast to wee baby Heather Margaret in the staff room at the end of the day when all the patients had gone home. Amid the good humour and happiness and a few damp eyes Jessica had found her own eyes drawn to Mike and surprised him watching her, an indefinable solemn look on his handsome face. Silently he had raised his glass in a toast to her and she had echoed his gesture. As they had both sipped the fizzy liquid she'd wondered if this was the moment to call a truce and, for a heart-stopping moment, believed that Mike thought the same as he'd looked as if he would move towards her. But then Graham had caught her by the arm and tugged her over to the others and the moment was lost. Never to be recaptured, it seemed.

'Not much to come now,' Jeannie informed Jessica optimistically as she searched the crowded room for space to unwrap the latest delivery. 'Everything should be here by the end of the week.'

In their planning they had left a whole week to hang the exhibition, which at that point had seemed more time than they could ever need. Now Jessica didn't think a month would be enough. How on earth were they going to manage? Sure, they could put things up on the walls, but it was only at this moment that Jessica was realising that that wouldn't make an exhibition. It had all seemed so easy at the start. When had it become so complicated?

'Jessie, can you come and see Hughie for me? I can't get him to calm down.' Graham's request was both the last straw and a means of saving her sanity.

Hughie had only spent a few weeks in hospital while his acute symptoms were brought under control through drugs and he was now back at the day hospital. Although by no means well, he was much better than he had been. As she went off to deal with Hughie, whose voices appeared to be getting out of control again, Jessica wondered if she could just run away from the whole enterprise. The sight of Hughie engaged in earnest but very loud conversation with the wall brought her to her senses. No matter how she felt, the patients came first.

Ten minutes later she had made a decision. There was no way she could practise medicine and organise the exhibition—not at this stage. Before she could change her mind she set off to see Mike.

'If it's all right with you,' she told the top of his head as he barely looked up from the papers in front of him on his desk, 'I'd like to take next week as holiday.'

That brought his head up with such a satisfying jerk that Jessica hoped he would suffer from whiplash. 'You what?'

'Want next week as a holiday. You see——'

'I see all right. I see that you've got more than you can handle with this exhibition and that it has all got beyond you. Well, let me tell you, Dr Balfour, that I always doubted your ability to stage this exhibition but I went along with it because everybody else seemed enthusiastic. Now you tell me you want a week off!

Throwing in the towel might be your usual way of getting out of situations where you've got yourself in over your head, but let me tell you. . .'

Jessica forced her mouth not to curve into a grin as Mike continued to rant at her, tripping himself up in his speech several times as his anger interfered with his capacity for coherent thought. You wait, Dr Michael Knight, she told him silently, I'll make you eat every single word. . .and then some!

'I think you misunderstood,' she finally interrupted him forcefully. 'Yes, I want next week as a holiday, but only because I've realised that I can't get this exhibition ready *and* practise psychiatry at the same time. I'm going to need to put all my energy into the preparation, and it's not fair to the patients—or to the exhibition, come to that—if I'm dashing from one to the other.'

'You want to take holiday, but you'll come in to sort out the current mess and get everything hung?'

'Got it in one!' Jessica didn't understand why she suddenly felt so much better, but it was as though a weight had been lifted from her shoulders. Most of it was due, she assumed, to the relief of knowing that with more time at her disposal she probably could sort things out, but not a little was due to the fact that, for once, she seemed to have silenced the opinionated Dr Knight.

'Don't you think that will cause confusion? If you're here, patients will want to see you. . .'

'Not if I explain it to them—tell them I'm not really here and they're to ignore me. Anyway, most of the time—for the first few days at least—I'll be in my room trying to get the pictures in some sort of order. And since I'll be in jeans and, no doubt, getting filthy, I'm sure they'll forget that I'm here.'

'Hmm.' Mike sounded sceptical, but she knew he didn't really have much choice. It was obvious to everyone that she couldn't do both things, and it would be easier if no one was expecting her to be working as a psychiatrist. 'I suppose you know what you're doing.' He didn't need to add that he didn't agree; his tone said all that was needed.

Her long legs clad in faded denim, an old baggy T-shirt coming down to the tops of her thighs and her hair caught back from her face in a banana slide, Jessica surveyed the row of paintings she had propped up along one of the long corridor walls early on this Saturday morning. The talent was impressive. Some of these were more than good—they were brilliant. Although, as was to be expected, most of the more technically able ones came from the professional artists and people with some artistic training, many of the ones that were crudely drawn or had little artistic skill were among the most powerful in demonstrating the artist's feelings about what had happened to them and what had been done to them.

She picked up a pencil drawing of men waiting for ECT and knew that she would have to buy it. The power embodied in the men was astonishing, given the desolation that the drawing conveyed. There was nothing comfortable about the picture and Jessica knew that she couldn't live with it in her home, but it would find pride of place on her office wall.

She contrasted it with the bright, primary colours swirling across a canvas—a picture of joy and exuberance until the swirls became whirlwinds of colour and any sense of control was lost, the painting becoming almost painful to look at. Turning it over, Jessica wasn't surprised to read that the woman who had painted it said it represented how being manic started out as exciting and fun, but how rapidly she lost control and then the nightmare began.

There was some work by relatives, and much of this concentrated on the burden of caring for someone with a chronic mental illness, although one mother had produced a series of pen-and-ink drawings juxtaposed with photographs to indicate how she saw her son, who had schizophrenia, withdrawing from the world into a friendless, apathetic world of his own where it was getting harder and harder to reach him.

A triptych of collages created by the patients and staff of an alcohol unit in another part of the city had been submitted. The OT who had organised the project had written an informative and amusing letter describing the breakdown in barriers between staff and patients as they had worked together to produce the panels depicting their lives and their fight against alcohol.

Very little work had come in from staff and she was disappointed by that, but not particularly surprised. Harry Smith had, true to his promise, completed a work entitled 'Breakdown of a Manager'. It was a very powerful oil-painting, it's comparative smallness seeming to heighten the emotions—emotions the frame was having difficulty containing.

'That's very good—who did it?' The unexpectedness of Mike's voice behind her caused Jessica to whirl round, a half stifled screech emerging from frozen lips at the same time as she lost her grip on the painting. In trying to save it from falling Mike made a grab for it and caught his finger on a loose piece of picture wire. 'Argh!' He let go of the picture, which crashed to the floor, its corner hitting him on the instep just as he was putting his bloody finger to his mouth.

Jessica felt that he could be forgiven the few swear words that escaped him then, but not the malevolent look he was casting in her direction.

'So help me, Jessica——' he began, but she wasn't going to let him get away with blaming her for his clumsiness.

'You're the one who crept up behind me and frightened me half out of my wits——'

'You don't have any wits to be frightened out of,' he told her, still sucking on his injured finger.

'—and then tried to grab the painting from me. What do you think you were trying to do?' Her lips twitched as she regarded the giant of a man before her who, at this precise moment, with his finger in his mouth, resembled nothing so much as a small boy looking for sympathy.

'What's funny?' he demanded gruffly, removing his finger from his mouth to inspect it for damage.

'Let me have a look,' Jessica suggested, stepping forward, 'I could always——' Her voice froze as she realised what she had been about to say. *I could always kiss it better.* That might be what mothers said to their small sons, but the last thing Jessica felt was maternal and she wanted to kiss very much more than his finger. Her colour rose but it seemed that all Mike had heard was the first part of her sentence, for now he was backing away from her, looking as though she were the four horsemen of the Apocalypse rolled into one shapely package.

'Stay away from me; you've done enough damage.'

Then, with injured dignity in every masculine line of his body, he stomped off to his office.

A few minutes later he was back with what to Jessica's jaundiced eye was an ostentatious and inappropriately large sticking-plaster on his finger and a bravely masked, and therefore unmistakable limp. He was getting no sympathy from her!

'If we're going to be working together much longer, I'm going to have to see about taking out more insurance.'

Definitely no sympathy.

'What are you doing here?'

As he was dressed similarly to her—only without the slide in his hair—Jessica deduced that he probably hadn't expected to run into anyone and had come in to catch up on some paperwork, which was confirmed by his next words.

'Paperwork. But what about you? I thought, with your "holiday" next week, you wouldn't need to be doing this now.'

Sighing, Jessica turned back to the paintings. 'I know, but then I thought I'd get peace and quiet today—'

'Instead of which you got me,' he interjected, causing Jessica to frown. Despite blaming her for his injuries, he was being very...matey...this morning and Jessica didn't trust him one little bit. So she carried on as though he hadn't spoken.

'—to lay everything out and see exactly what there is. With everybody in during the day, it's going to be difficult to get things sorted out. I want to get some idea of how to group things and maybe get some of the stuff moved into the right rooms ready to be hung and—'

'Whoa there!' Mike held up his hands in surrender. 'You've convinced me how much there is to do. I guess the paperwork can wait one more day. What do you want me to do?'

'Do?' Jessica couldn't take in what he was saying. Or maybe it was that she didn't want to take in what he was saying. These last few months she had got used to seeing him on an almost daily basis and had learnt to keep her feelings under tight control. That didn't mean those feelings had gone away, though, and if he continued to be this friendly—she wouldn't believe it was flirting—then she didn't think she was going to get through the rest of the morning.

'Yes, *do*, Jessica. I might not have much of an artistic eye, but I can move things around for you. Are you bringing everything out of your office?'

'Er. . .yes. Well. . .not everything. . .just so I can get some idea. . .I mean. . .we need to see everything. . .and. . .er. . .'

'I get the picture,' Mike told her and then winced at his unintended pun. 'I'll start pulling stuff out and you tell me where to stack it.'

An hour later they were surveying two long lines of paintings stretching the length of the corridor, and Jessica felt utterly beaten. Mike had proved to be totally uncomplaining as she'd got him to move paintings around, propping them against the wall, and she'd tried to get some idea of how things would look grouped together.

Frantically she tried to remember the advice that Alison from the art gallery had given her, but it was no good. None of it made any sense and Jessica knew herself beaten and shamingly close to tears. She waited for Mike to say 'I told you so' but, uncharacteristically, she thought, he was silent. In fact he seemed to have forgotten her and the exhibition altogether, standing lost in thought.

Coming back to the present from wherever he had been, he raised an expressive eyebrow before fully taking in Jessica's woebegone face. 'What's wrong, now?' he asked in surprisingly gentle tones, and that was nearly her undoing.

Shrugging, she strove for mastery of her voice as she answered. 'It's hopeless. I don't know what I'm doing. I never did. Why I thought I could organise an art exhibition I'll never know. The whole thing is a shambles and——'

Mike cut in, breaking off her rising hysteria, 'It's not as bad as all that, surely? Some of this work is truly outstanding and the power and emotion in much of it is——'

'I know, I know. That's half the problem. Some of it's fantastic and some of it—not much, I grant you—is terrible. How can it all go together? We said we'd hang everything, so we can't get rid of any. And then the work that is good is *so* good that I feel we're not going to do justice to it, and. . .' Her voice was rising again and Mike took further steps to stop the rising panic.

'Calm down.' He came and put a comforting arm round her shoulders, which did absolutely nothing to calm her rapidly running out of control emotions and sent the colour flooding her cheeks again and her heart-rate up alarmingly.

'I thought you said Naomi was going to help you decide where everything was to go.'

For a moment the mention of the OT brought calm, but then Jessica recalled what Naomi had said to her. 'I'll give you all the help I can, you know that, Jessie, but it's not really my thing. I've never been involved in an exhibition like this before. It's really up to you.'

That didn't exactly inspire her with confidence.

'Ye-e-s.' Dragging the word out, Jessica indicated to Mike that maybe he shouldn't place too much reliance on the other woman's skills either.

'Are you telling me. . .' He dropped his arm and took a step back. 'No, don't bother. I might have known. Who are you expecting to get you out of your mess this time?'

Whatever friendly atmosphere there had been between them vanished as the emotional temperature dropped several degrees and shields were once again raised.

'Morning, Doctor, enjoying your holiday?' Maggie stood watching Jessica, rocking backwards and forwards slightly from the balls of her feet to her heels, her hands thrust into the pockets of an old and shapeless cardigan, a beatific smile on her crumpled face.

The idea that Jessica was there but not there, so to speak, had caused a great deal of amusement among the patients, but they all appeared to be adapting to the idea well enough. They might be talking to her, and offering advice on what pictures should go where, but not once did anybody mention anything pertaining to psychiatry or their illness. Even Hughie had walked past demanding to talk to a doctor and deliberately averting his head when he saw Jessica in the corridor. The gesture had touched her deeply and she could have hugged him.

'Dr Balfour?'

Jessica straightened and looked up into greeny blue eyes the colour of the sea off the west coast and, by the twinkle in them, just as dangerous. Jessica knew that she didn't know this young man in his early twenties but all the same there was something vaguely familiar about him. Thick mousy brown hair fell over his forehead and curled on to the collar of his shirt and his mouth stretched into a wide smile.

'Yes, I'm Dr Balfour.' She admitted the information grudgingly. If he was someone's relative she didn't really have time to deal with him now. Added to which, her faded jeans and baggy shirt didn't bode very well for a professional relationship.

His grin broadened further. 'Now I see what all the urgency was about.'

'And you are?' She waited for him to introduce himself and thought she caught a glimpse of surprise in his eyes.

'Jake.'

'Jake?'

The surprise was definite this time. 'You mean you're not expecting me?' The comically dismayed look on his face made him look younger, but did nothing to dispel his charm.

'Should I be?' He might be young and good-looking but Jessica didn't have time to stand around in idle chat. Over the weekend she had decided that there was nothing for it but to plough on with the exhibition and just do the best that she could. Now she didn't want anything distracting her from that task. And this young man could certainly be distracting if he put his mind to it, that was for sure.

'After dragging me away from my work, I would have thought——' the young man called Jake began, then, as though realising Jessica wasn't the one he was annoyed with, switched on his sunny smile again and held out his hand. 'Jake Knight. Nephew of Dr Michael Knight and here at my dear uncle's request to give you a hand with the exhibition.'

'Oh. Fine.' What was she supposed to say? It would be useful to have a young man around to do the lifting and carrying but Jessica wasn't sure that she wanted to have to work so closely with someone else when she was so uncertain about what she was doing herself.

'Ah, I see you've met Jake.' Mike appeared out of his room and beamed at them both, as though he had just done something very clever. 'I thought he might give you a hand and——'

'Yes. It's very kind of you to think of it—and of you to offer,' she added, turning to Jake, 'but I don't think. . .'

Jake clearly wasn't listening, but was looking down the corridor in both directions and glancing back down the stairs. 'What other space have you got?' he demanded abruptly, then, looking at Mike, 'You said something about a couple of big rooms and. . .' He loped off down the corridor, clearly expecting them to follow.

'I thought you'd be pleased.'

Jessica couldn't decide whether Mike sounded put out and irritated or put out and hurt at her lack of enthusiasm for the help of his nephew, but it was more than she could cope with.

'I said it's good of you both, but I don't think I can——'

'After what you said on Saturday I thought you'd find his experience useful and——'

It was Jessica's turn to interrupt. 'What experience?'

Mike's face cleared as light began to dawn. 'Didn't he explain?' he enquired with false innocence.

Life suddenly began to look more hopeful. 'No, he didn't. And neither did you! What experience?'

'Jake graduated from the art school last year. His mother has run an art gallery in the city for many years and Jake has helped out there ever since he was big enough to carry a hammer or lift a painting. He's been putting in quite a bit of time this last year while——'

Jessica didn't wait to hear any more. 'Jake. . .' She was off down the corridor after him.

'What do you think?' Jake had taken Jessica off to the pub for lunch and a 'strategy meeting' as he termed it. Neither of them had missed the disapproval in Mike's eyes, but no one had said anything.

'The truth?'

'The truth.'

'To be honest, it's not as bad as I thought it was going to be. You've got some wonderful stuff and some of the space isn't bad. Of course a lot of the lighting is awful, but we'll just have to work with what there is. The corridors could prove quite useful and I think the stairwell will work surprisingly well. Of course everything you've put up so far will have to come down.'

Jessica gave a passing regret to all the hard work she had put in on Saturday, after Mike had left, hanging work in the day-room, but let the thought go without a qualm.

'Fine. Whatever you say.'

'Fine?' Jake sounded as though he hadn't expected her capitulation to be that easy.

'You obviously know what you're doing. It's also equally obvious that I really haven't got a clue. I'll go along with anything you say.'

'Anything?' Jake's unsuccessful attempt at a leer only caused Jessica to feel even more confident.

'Almost anything,' she amended with a grin.

'I can't think why Uncle Mike thought you might be difficult,' Jake commented, just as that man came into view.

'Is this a private meeting or can anyone join in?' he asked, sitting down before either of the other two could answer him.

CHAPTER EIGHT

THE next couple of days passed in a whirlwind of activity that had Jessica dropping into bed at night too tired to think, let alone worry over Mike's recent behaviour. He had joined them in the pub for lunch and, so it had seemed to Jessica, had done his best to cut Jake out of the conversation. If his nephew had known what Mike was doing he'd given no evidence of it, but had turned the tables on his uncle by insisting that they talk about the exhibition, art in general, and a series of ever more unlikely mishaps as he'd recounted his years at the art school and his time working for his mother. At last Mike had left them in disgust, muttering something under his breath about some of them having work to do.

Jake had just grinned and waved him off with a, 'Bye, Uncle Mike', which had brought an even fiercer scowl to that man's already furrowed brow. The scowl appeared to have become a permanent fixture by the time they'd returned to the hospital and Mike's mood had looked as though it was deteriorating rapidly. It had not been improved by one of Maggie's famously outrageous observations.

She had been waiting for Jessica and Jake as they returned and she'd waylaid Jake, who had taken the inspection of his person in good part. Mike had 'just happened' to be passing and stopped to hear Maggie's pronouncement with barely concealed amusement. The amusement hadn't lasted long, however.

Having carefully eyed Jake up and down, Maggie had delivered her verdict. 'You're a fine-looking lad. You'll outshine your uncle when you're full-grown.'

Naomi, who had arrived just in time to hear this, had spluttered and beaten a hasty retreat, while Jessica had done her best to muffle the laughter which had threatened to overwhelm her. Jake, twenty-two years old and six feet three, had been torn between delight at going one better than Uncle Mike and dismay at almost being dismissed as a child. Mike had simply looked thunderstruck. The sight of Jessica choking back her laughter had turned his expression to anger and he'd stalked off, his rigid back defeating any attempt he might have made to shrug the incident off. Why, Jessica wondered, had Maggie's comment annoyed him so? He had taken coming second to Nathan Pride in good part.

That Jake knew what he was doing in arranging the exhibition had become evident once they'd returned to the hospital. He'd had Jessica and a couple of the male patients take everything down from the walls and then he'd spent what seemed an inordinate amount of time wandering up and down, shifting paintings about as they rested on the walls, deep in thought, his hands continually raking his hair until it stood on end. Then, with a lightning change of mood, he'd had them running up and down stairs and the length of the hospital as he'd started to move paintings into place.

After the first few days Jessica's heart soared as she began to believe that Jake really was going to perform miracles and something resembling an exhibition started to take shape. A large square where the corridor widened out became a sculpture gallery with several of the larger paintings on the wall. With only a couple of days to go to the grand opening, Jessica was breathing a little easier.

'Let's go out for lunch; we deserve it.' A brief break for sandwiches was all Jake had allowed for the past two days, and Jessica was only too thankful to down tools for an hour and get out of the hospital. She was fed up with measuring pictures, walls and hanging-spaces, with knocking picture-pins into the wall and then finding that the picture was out of line. Jake was shaping up to outdo his uncle in the autocratic stakes, Jessica had long ago decided, as that young man told her yet again that something was an inch out and she would have to adjust the picture wire. Her fingers were sore from pulling wire and cord through rings and tightening it until the master was satisfied.

The weather had been getting hotter as the week progessed and Jessica felt hot and sweaty in her old jeans and T-shirt, not to say a little dusty and grimy round the edges, but the thought of a cooling glass of white wine was enough to send her rushing for a quick wash and brush-up before they set off for the pub.

As they crossed the car park Jessica had the strange sensation of eyes boring into her. She risked a quick glance over her shoulder, but there was no one in sight. Something made her raise her eyes and she encountered Mike watching them from his office window. Though she was too far away to see his expression, the set of his head and shoulders was enough to tell her he was annoyed.

'It's good of your mother to spare you,' Jessica told Jake when he had grudgingly fetched her a white wine. He didn't want her drunk or sleepy, he had told her, with no trace of teasing, so after that it was going to be orange juice.

'The exhibition she has at the moment is going well. I was surplus to requirements, or so she said.'

Jessica still found it very odd that Mike had never mentioned his sister-in-law in all the times they had discussed the exhibition. She could have offered so much advice. If he had wanted to keep his family well out of it, why bring Jake into it now? She wanted to ask Jake about it, but didn't know how to broach the subject.

'I don't know why Mike didn't rope me in earlier, or Mum, come to that.' It seemed that Jake had no qualms about commenting on his uncle's odd behaviour. Jessica also noticed how he dropped the 'uncle' when he referred to Mike. She was beginning to realise that the 'Uncle Mike' was both for her benefit and to annoy Mike. That it *did* annoy him was evident from his permanent scowl.

'Maybe he thought I knew what I was doing.'

Jessica didn't need Jake to choke into his lager and raise his eyebrows heavenwards to know that her sentiment wasn't very likely.

'All right, there's no need to look like that,' she informed him a trifle irritably. What was it with these Knight men that made them want to see her as an incompetent? 'He probably wanted to see me fall flat on my face.' She didn't realise how despondent she sounded at that and, gazing into her nearly empty glass of wine as though that could give her the answer, missed the quick, concerned look Jake gave her.

'Why bring me in, then?' he asked reasonably, but Jessica just shrugged.

'The great Dr Michael Knight saves the day again,'

she hazarded, knowing she sounded bitter and not caring. 'It's good for his image, wouldn't you say? Rescuing another stupid woman who thought she could do something.'

Jake took the wine glass from her unresisting fingers and put it on the table before demanding, 'Jessica, look at me.' His tone was so serious that she had complied before she had had a chance to think, and saw that although his face matched his tone there was a twinkle in his eyes that belied the serious message. 'I think there's maybe something you need to know about Mike.' He stopped abruptly. 'Maybe not. If he hasn't told you, there must be a reason. All I'll say is that, my mum apart, the women in the family have been a bit——' He stopped abruptly, realising he was getting in deeper by the minute. 'Well. . .helpless,' he continued after a pause. 'It's left all the men a bit jaundiced. I remember Mike telling me not to trust helpless women from the time I was tiny.'

'It doesn't seem to have affected you,' Jessica retorted sharply, remembering how he had had her running around like a skivvy all week.

'When you meet my mum you'll understand why,' he told her. 'A very determined lady, my mum.' He grinned. 'If you want my advice,' Jake continued smugly, 'and you're going to get it whether you do or not, you'll hang in there and show Mike what you're made of. He's losing ground already.'

'I don't know what you mean!' Her face scarlet, Jessica turned away, but not before she had seen the broad grin of Jake's face.

'I think you do. Otherwise, as I said, why bring me in?'

Jessica shook her head. 'You don't understand. I've

done nothing but show Mike how useless and accident-prone I am ever since we met. He thinks I'm totally helpless.' In the face of Jake's certainty there didn't seem any point in denying her attraction to Mike. And somehow, without being able to put it into words, she knew that she could trust Jake not to tell Mike.

'Then you just have to prove that you're not, don't you?' he said, with all the confidence of youth that it was that easy

'Why don't you go home now and get yourself tidied up for tonight? You look all in.'

Jessica knew that she looked tired and scruffy, but to have Mike point it out so bluntly did nothing for her flagging spirits. Something in the droop of her shoulders must have indicated to Mike that he had been less than tactful for he added quickly, 'You've been working hard and done a really wonderful job here. It would be a shame if you were too tired to enjoy the grand opening.'

'But there's still the——'

'Nothing we can't handle,' Mike insisted.

Secretly exhausted, both physically and mentally, Jessica was desperate to get home and put her feet up for an hour before having to come back and act the hostess to the great and the good at the preview they were having to launch the exhibition.

'Stuart can give a hand laying out the glasses and wine.'

Jessica sighed. Stuart had been notably absent all week when any help was required but although she hadn't expected much help from the other staff—they were, after all, still trying to work and deal with the patients—they had all chipped in when they had had a free moment. Not Stuart, though. Apart from offering a few words of 'advice' at odd moments, always when no one else was about to hear him, he had kept well out of her way.

'Go home, Jessie.' There was something so gentle, almost tender, in Mike's tone that she could do nothing but obey. His parting words stunned her, though, as she reached the door. 'I'll pick you up at five-thirty.'

She turned to look at him, her peaty brown eyes huge in her surprised face, but all he said was another, 'Go home.'

It was amazing what a long soak in a warm bath with bubbles caressing her shoulders and spilling over the sides could do, Jessica noted as she wrapped herself in a fluffy towel and sat down in front of her dressing-table to do her make-up. It was too hot to wear much and she contented herself with accetuating her eyes with brown and amber shadow and several coats of mascara, making her eyelashes impossibly long. Deep coral lipstick enhanced her mouth and nothing else was necessary. Ruthlessly she swept her hair up on top of her head and then spent long minutes coaxing the wayward curls to fall in just the right degree of abandon from where thay had been anchored.

She had debated long and hard with herself about what she should wear. Regretfully she put aside a soft, filmy dress in a cream print on white lawn in favour of a tailored linen dress in deep amber. It was, after all, a work event and she wanted to maintain her professional image. And maybe the floaty dress was just a bit too helpless-looking, an insistent little voice added.

It was really too hot to want to wear tights, yet bare legs would look as though she was going to the beach.

And she wasn't sure how comfortable her beige court shoes would be without them. Inspiration struck as she remembered a pair of hold-up stockings she had bought but never worn. What better occasion? Quickly she donned them and was admiring herself in the mirror when the doorphone went.

Quickly she went to let Mike in and then, leaving the door open, went back into her bedroom for her handbag and jacket. The stockings felt odd, unused as she was to feeling the elastic gripping her thighs, and she hurriedly made sure they were well pulled up.

By the time she had walked down the stairs, she was beginning to think she had made a mistake. The stockings didn't feel at all secure. She wondered about asking Mike to wait while she made some excuse to go back and change, but he was already holding the car door open and murmuring that they had better get a move on if they were to get to the hospital before the guests.

Half way to the hospital Jessica knew that she was going to have to do something. Visions of her stockings slowly sliding down her legs as the evening progressed filled her imagination. Even if things didn't get as bad as that, she knew that she would be on edge all evening unless she changed.

'Stop here, will you?' she asked Mike, clutching at his sleeve and causing him to swear mildly as he lost his concentration in the heavy traffic.

'Why?' he demanded, although he was already slowing.

Not giving him an answer, she rushed into the corner shop and bought a pair of tights. They only had one-size ones and, being tall, she just hoped that they would be long enough and would not start to descend as well!

Back in the car, she clutched the tights in her hand but said nothing. Easing the car back into the stream of traffic, Mike cast her a cautious look. 'Are you going to tell me what that was all about?'

Firmly she shook her head, but the colour that tinted her cheeks told of some embarrassing story. It was with some surprise that she thankfully accepted Mike's non-committal, 'Hmm,' followed by, 'You can tell me later.'

The unfortunate stockings discarded and the new tights in their place, Jessica joined Mike to receive their guests. Wine was upstairs and they directed everyone upwards to where Naomi was waiting to give them a catalogue and point them towards a drink.

Jessica had sent out several hundred invitations to all kinds of people ranging from the high and mighty at the health board and mental health unit, consultants from St Mungo's, all heads of departments and people who had been involved to local councillors and people from the local art world—anyone they thought might conceivably have an interest or be of potential benefit to the day hospital. All the patients from the day hospital who had paintings on show or who had helped had been invited, and although most of them had chosen to absent themselves a few were making the rounds, proudly showing off their work.

A lot of the work was for sale and Jessica found herself busy sticking a gratifyingly large number of red dots on paintings and taking cheques from people who had maybe come out of curiosity, but had bought out of real appreciation.

'Well done, Jessie.'
'Congratulations, Jessica.'
'Good job, Dr Balfour.'
'Never thought it was going to be so grand.'
'Splendid, my dear.'

The words of praise came thick and fast and Jessica knew they had a success on their hands. She scrupulously credited Jake with hanging the work and making it look like a 'real' exhibition and included the other members of staff in her comments about how hard they had all worked, but everyone knew it had been her idea and her enthusiasm which had carried the project to completion.

Jake wandered round looking very artistic in head-to-toe black, pleased with what he had achieved but not trying to take any of the limelight from Jessica. She was introduced to his father, Forbes, and to his mother, Caroline. Forbes looked like an older version of Mike, but a couple of inches shorter and with a less determined chin. Jessica took to him on sight. Caroline was a total surprise, being tiny and very blonde with a delicate air about her. Two minutes in her company, however, dispelled any image of the 'little woman' and it was clear that she had a mind of her own and wasn't to be cowed by the giants of men in her life. If anything, they looked as though they would do her bidding without question.

Hughie, who for once appeared to have his voices under some sort of control, was standing by his sculpture, which was an abstract representation of his views on medication, holding forth to an interested and respectful audience.

Jeannie was rushing around, face flushed, glass of white wine firmly clutched in one hand, while she made sure that catalogues were being distributed and encouraged visitors to sign the visitors' book. She looked as though she was thoroughly in control and, what was even better, was thoroughly enjoying herself. She flushed even pinker when the chairman of the health board introduced himself and praised her for the good work she had put in.

'I don't think he realises I'm a patient,' she whispered worriedly to Jessica.

'Does it matter?' Jessica whispered back conspiratorially. 'You've done a good job. Accept the praise. Enjoy yourself.'

'You're right,' Jeannie confirmed with more confidence and, before Jessica could add anything else, the other woman had launched herself back into the fray.

Several local journalists and their photographers turned up and Jessica heard herself sounding intelligent and lucid as she talked to them without having the first idea of what she was saying. She had one photograph taken by one of the sculptures, another by a dramatic black and white painting which had a number of violent images featuring in it, and then one with Mike as they looked at a collage made from cigarette packets by one of their patients. It was inevitable, Jessica supposed, that it was the only female photographer who insisted on having Mike in the photo.

Not that she minded. By then she was too dazed to mind anything very much. She had downed a couple a glasses of wine which, coupled with the overwhelming sense of relief and an empty stomach, made her feel as though she was floating a couple of inches above the ground.

'Come on, let's go.' Mike caught her round the waist, steadying her as she stumbled.

'Can't go. Clearing up to do.' Her tongue felt very slightly too large for her mouth and the words came out less distinctly than she would have liked.

'Everyone's gone except our staff and a few people from St Mungo's. I think they're going to stay on and have a go at finishing the wine. I get the feeling they'd be happier if we went.'

'But——'

'Don't argue, there's a good girl.'

'I'm not a girl. . .' Jessica began indignantly, her words fading away as she took note of the look in Mike's eye as he muttered,

'No, you're not, are you?'

Without further argument she allowed herself to be led out to his car, was gently pushed in and ten minutes later was being ushered into a quiet restaurant in the merchant city.

'You haven't eaten properly all day and need something to soak up the wine,' Mike told her, forestalling any objection she might make.

Sinking back on to the banquette, Jessica accepted that she didn't want to make any objection, after all. She was going to get to have some time with Mike and maybe they could put their past difference behind them in the heady success of the exhibition.

Later she couldn't remember what they ate, only that Mike had kept her wine glass full and that they had laughed a lot. He had even got out of her the embarrassing story of her hold-up stockings which wouldn't hold-up. Although he had laughed as she had explained what had happened he had ended up shaking his head, more in resignation than anything else.

'It could only happen to you,' he had told her ruefully and, although he had smiled when he said it,

Jessica had detected an underlying disapproval in his words.

The memory of the journey back to her flat was hazy, but she did have a vague image of Mike helping her up the stairs and pushing her into a chair in her living-room before making them both coffee.

'You're almost asleep.' His words came through a misty fog, as though from a great distance, and she murmured words of protest. She didn't want him to go. She felt his hands take hers as he pulled her to her feet. 'Go to bed, Jessica. I'll see myself out.'

'No.' Her answer was a muffled moan as she stumbled forward and was caught against Mike's broad chest and held tight for a second before he took a step back. That wasn't what Jessica wanted at all and she leant forward, her hands splayed across his shirt-front as she slid them upwards to his shoulders.

With a groan somewhere deep in his throat Mike pulled her forward, his head coming down as his lips covered hers with a hard swiftness that had Jessica swept along on a tide of rising passion. His hand caught the back of her head, holding her in place while his tongue teased at her lips, persuading them to open so that it could slip inside her mouth, causing Jessica's knees to buckle as she sagged against him.

Mike stooped to catch her and picked her up as though she weighed no more than a child, carrying her through to lay her on her bed. As Jessica would have reached for him again he straightened and moved out of reach. 'You've had too much to drink, which, coupled with your success tonight, means you're in no position to make a sensible decision. So I'll make it for you. Go to sleep, Jessica.'

'But I——'

'You'll hate yourself tomorrow,' he told her with a certainty which shocked her. 'And anyway, when we make love for the first time I want you to be sober. Not saying you didn't know what you were doing.'

And before she could find anything to say or do to keep him with her he had gone.

He was right, she thought the next morning as she blearily faced a glass of orange juice, I would have hated myself this morning. And I would have said I didn't know what I was doing. None of which meant that she still didn't regret his leaving.

All morning she waited for his call because, after what they had shared, she was sure he *would* call. By the afternoon she was getting edgy and by teatime she had given up. Maybe Sunday. But no call came and she was forced to accept that what had been so special for her had meant nothing to him.

Jake called to congratulate her on her success and to receive his own warm congratulations from her. At his insistence she arranged to meet him for lunch during the week, but talking to Jake only made her miss Mike more. Sunday night she cried herself to sleep, the realisation that she loved him overwhelming her. She had always thought that when she fell in love it would be heady and exciting, that it would colour every part of her life with happiness and expectation. The reality was so different. Her love lay like a leaden weight on her heart, filling her with depression and despair. Far from enhancing her life it made everything seem pointless, worthless.

Monday morning saw her made of sterner stuff. Mike had given her the perfect way out. She could blame her actions on a heady mixture of alcohol and euphoria and put it behind her. He had made it abundantly clear that he wasn't interested in her. The fact that he had talked of making love to her, she concluded, belonged in some wish-fulfilment dream.

CHAPTER NINE

'SEE me, Nurse. That's my picture there. Sold.' The somewhat dishevelled man stood proudly by his painting while the young nurse took his photograph. He was probably younger than he looked, the careworn lines etched on his face adding to his years, but now he stood taller, straighter than when he had walked into the hospital.

One of the things that had given Jessica the most satisfaction was seeing the effect having their pictures shown in a 'proper exhibition' had had on people whose confidence had been sorely undermined by mental health problems. A number of paitents hadn't priced their work, believing that no one would want it, that it wasn't good enough. Some of it, certainly, was unlikely to sell but others had already had enquiries made about them. Many of the patients now had the confidence to start putting a price to their work.

The man who was now standing so proudly with his haunting picture of depression had sold his at the opening. Looking at him, Jessica found it hard to believe that he had painted something so moving and chided herself for making snap, prejudiced judgements.

'Are you having tea?' Graham was moving in the direction of the big coffee-room and stopped to have a word with Jessica.

'No, I don't think so. Mrs Morris's husband's been

on the phone again, so I'd better go down there and see what's going on.'

'You know it'll only be a false alarm.'

'I know. But one day. . . Well, you can't be too sure, can you?'

'Suppose not.' Graham shrugged and continued on his way.

As the work of the day hospital had to go on normally the exhibition was only open in the evenings and at weekends. But there had been so many requests from other hospitals to bring groups of patients that two days a week the day-hospital patients hosted an 'at home', as Maggie called it, dispensing tea and cakes to their visitors while showing them round the exhibition. The original idea had been Jeannie's and she was doing most of the organising.

At least I was right there, Jessica thought to herself. Jeannie's come on by leaps and bounds. She had even managed to push her uncooperative mother into a taxi to bring her down to see the exhibition. Mrs MacPherson might not have had a lot to say but Jessica had noticed the older woman taking in how much everyone was praising Jeannie for all her hard work. Jessica had also noticed that Mrs MacPherson hadn't liked that. Now that Jeannie's confidence had grown so much maybe the time was approaching when they would have to tackle seriously the problem of her relationship with her mother.

'I thought Graham was on duty tonight.' Jessica stared at Mike in consternation. She had managed to avoid him all week, without raising too much suspicion, by finding a lot of patients who needed to see her at home, which got her out of the way when she wasn't in clinics.

Staff from the day hospital and St Mungo's acted as guides and wardens for the exhibition. To cover the whole building it really needed four of them, but sometimes the rota got down to two. Tonight was one of those nights.

'I swapped with him,' Mike told her cheerfully. 'Something about a date with the new OT at St Mungo's. Seems they met when they shared a duty at the weekend.' His grin was positively devilish. 'Do you think sharing this time together will have the same effect on us?'

Yes, her heart wanted to say. No, her head was insisting. What she might have answered she was never to know, for at that moment the door was pushed open and three scruffy boys walked in. They were all short, but Jessica guessed their ages to be between eight and ten.

Mike looked down at them from his great height, one eyebrow lifted interrogatively.

'We want to see the pictures—that all right?' The youngest one dared Mike to make a question of his statement, dared him to say they couldn't come in.

For a tense moment Jessica thought Mike was going to order them out of the building, but then his stance relaxed and he nodded. 'Sure.' He handed them a catalogue, even though all the pictures were labelled, and pointed them in the direction of the 'sculpture-room'.

As they watched them turn the corner Mike sighed. 'I guess I had better go and keep a discreet eye on them.' Casually he tossed a fifty-pence coin into the cash box. 'For the catalogue,' he said in response to Jessica's blank look, and sauntered off after their unlikely trio of visitors.

Not long after a family of tourists from the south of England arrived, and Jessica was busy explaining the layout to them.

'My sister has trouble with her nerves,' the woman confided, out of earshot of her teenage children. 'So when we saw the poster for this I thought. . .well. . . we might learn something.'

A lot of the people who came to the exhibition had had trouble with their nerves in the past, or had someone in the family who was or had been ill. The power of many of the pictures was sometimes their undoing and the staff had learnt that some people needed to talk before they could leave, to share some of their feelings. Sometimes they recounted past sorrows, but they all praised the exhibition and the work it was doing in helping people understand some of the pain, the uncertainty, the dilemmas of psychological problems.

Naomi had told her only that day how a mother had explained that seeing paintings and other work by a number of people with schizophrenia, who addressed the issues of the illness in their paintings, had helped her realise that her son really *didn't* have control over his odd ideas.

None of the work indicated whether it had come from a patient, relative or staff, although some of the explanations or subject matter made it clear. Harry Smith had been perversely pleased to hear two people discussing his *Breakdown of a Manager*, assuming him to be someone who was 'very sick'.

'I knew I was working too hard,' he'd told Jessica cheerfully. 'Now I have proof.'

'Coffee?' Mike broke into her thoughts, placing a mug of milky instant in front of her.

'Thanks.' Did he have to stand so close? Just having him perched on the side of the table, his legs inches from her, brought her out in a mild panic. This is adolescent, she told herself, but the information didn't do anything to change the situation. Looking up, she watched as his lips twisted in a lazy grin, but all she could remember was the feel of them on hers, the slight rasp of his chin, in need of a shave.

'What's happened to the three boys?' She hadn't seen them leave, so presumably they were still in the building somewhere. It seemed a bit of a risk leaving them alone.

'They're in the corridor upstairs,' Mike replied with an unconcerned shrug. 'Other people are up there so I don't think they'll get into any trouble.' He stopped and frowned. 'In fact they've behaved impeccably. They're going round and actually looking at the paintings and things properly. And having discussions about them.' He shook his head. 'That'll teach me to jump to conclusions.'

'I thought the same,' Jessica confessed and they shared a shamefaced grin, a grin that served to defuse the tension between them, and Jessica at once felt more relaxed.

'You're giving a paper at the rehab conference at the end of the week,' Mike commented, taking Jessica by surprise with his sudden change of subject. Before she had time to do more that nod he continued, 'I'm going too, so we can travel down together.'

The conference was being held at a hotel on the west coast. Although it would only take an hour and a half or so to get there, that was an hour and a half too much for Jessica.

'Oh, I was——' She wasn't allowed to finish.

'The journey will give us time to do some work.' He grinned his lazy grin again. 'It's surprising how much you can achieve on a car journey if you put your mind to it.'

And that could be taken in several ways, Jessica realised, just as she was about to agree with him. But, whatever she said, it didn't look as though she was to get out of going with Mike. In which case she might as well give in and enjoy it.

A clatter of footsteps down the stairs intruded into the suddenly tense silence and the three boys came into sight. They slowed their progress as they approached the two adults. Jessica rose from her chair and smiled at them.

'Did you enjoy it?'

'Aye.'

'Dead brilliant.'

The two older ones moved away towards the visitors' book but the smallest boy, who was quite cute-looking when you really looked at him, Jessica noticed, stayed where he was, smiling shyly at her.

'My gran comes here most days,' he confided in a whisper. 'It isn't so bad, is it?' And then, as though overcome by his own boldness at the admission, he let out a whoop and took off at a run out of the building and into the bright early evening sunlight, followed by his two friends.

It was worth it, Jessica thought. If for nothing else than that comment, it was worth it. Mike was giving her a very strange look and she realised that she had a soppy grin on her face and her eyes were bright with unshed tears. Mike hadn't heard the comment and she knew she would have to get herself under a bit more control before she could tell him.

He had, however, presumably given up on emotional females because he was frowning at the visitors' book, which the two boys had been poring over, laboriously writing something. 'If it's too bad we can always tear the page out,' he was muttering as he picked it up. His frown deepened for a second as he read what had been written, then his face became completely neutral as he handed the book to Jessica.

'Brilliant' had been traced out in very uncertain letters by one of them and the 'dead good' of the other was hardly better. Writing was clearly not one of their skills. Jessica felt the tears threaten once again and had the suspicion that Mike was also looking slightly too bright around the eyes.

'What was I saying about prejudice and jumping to conclusions?' he muttered, carefully placing the book back on the table.

If Jessica had hoped that he would suggest a drink or a meal when their shift ended she was to be disappointed. With a cheery wave he left her at her car in the car park and walked on to his own without a backward glance. So much for the shared duty bringing them together.

'Turn right here.' Jessica frowned at the map in front of her, having real difficulty in marrying the crisscrossing streets on it with the actuality through which they were driving. She was only too thankful that Mike swung the car in the direction she had indicated without question. Trying not to draw attention to what she was doing, she turned the roughly drawn map around until she thought it was orientated in the direction they were travelling.

–'Right again.'

Mike cast a quick glance at her but again turned the car in the direction she gave, although his frown was now matching Jessica's.

'Left here.'

The car slowed, and cornered. 'Are you sure?'

'Yes.' She tried to sound positive. 'Yes, I'm sure.'

'I thought the hotel was further west than this.'

West! What did he mean, west? By now Jessica was having problems keeping left and right straight, and she had no idea which direction was west. It took all her time to remember that north wasn't automatically straight ahead!

'It's not much further now,' she asserted confidently, then spoilt it by adding a very hesitant, 'I think.'

They drove in silence for a few minutes, crossing several roads, before Jessica abruptly announced, 'Right here.'

'Right?' Mike sounded openly sceptical and this time, rather than following her directions, slowed the car to a halt by the side of the road. Without a word he took the diagram that had been sent to them by the conference organisers directing them to the hotel, turned it so that it was the right way round, glanced at it briefly and, without a word, put the car in gear and set off, swinging the car into a graceful U-turn to retrace the last part of their journey. As he sent the car round a corner Jessica, stunned by his behaviour, came back to life.

'Shouldn't we turn left here?' she asked, her hands indicating a clear right turn.

Again Mike slowed the car to a halt, and this time turned to face her. His face was entirely serious as he looked at her, but there was a teasing light in his eyes as he spoke. 'Jessica, you are good at many things, but navigating isn't one of them. Now, just be a good girl and shut up.'

Speechless, Jessica could only watch him as he drove off. The journey was finished swiftly, and in an entirely different direction from the one in which Jessica had been pointing them, in silence. Much as she wanted to challenge him, to find some way of overcoming his smugly superior stance, she couldn't. She *was* a hopeless navigator. Left to herself she didn't know where they would have ended up, but it wouldn't have been the conference hotel. The final straw came when, having reached their destination and unloaded their bags from the boot, Mike grinned at her and muttered, 'Good girl,' as he followed her into the hotel foyer.

Sipping her sherry, Jessica tried to decide whether she was annoyed, confused, disappointed or what. The only conclusion she could come to was that she was all three, and if the 'or what' translated as frustrated she was that as well. She and Mike had driven down in glorious sunshine that morning and, true to his word, they had completed a lot of work on the journey, discussing proposals for a planned reorganisation of service delivery while Jessica jotted down notes for the report Mike would be putting in to the unit manager. Once they'd arrived at the conference hotel he had ignored her.

Mike's room was several doors away from hers, towards the end of a corridor. He had watched her unlock her door from the safe distance of his, but not so far that she couldn't see the superior smirk of his face. He hadn't said a word, although she'd known they were both recalling a certain scene in a London hotel. Cheeks burning, Jessica had been relieved to be safely out of his sight.

She'd joined some people she knew sitting under the big umbrellas on the terrace outside the bar, only half her attention on the gossip about people who weren't coming or who hadn't arrived yet. She knew without seeing him when Mike came out on to the terrace, the hairs on the back of her neck standing on end, but was disappointed that he didn't join them. Instead he joined people at a table further down, and Jessica felt a stab of jealousy knife through her as an attractive blonde woman leapt to her feet to hug him warmly. It was a few seconds before the mist of jealousy lifted from her eyes and she saw that the woman was Dr Rowan Stewart and that the man now shaking Mike warmly by the hand was her husband, Dr Nathan Pride. Jessica recalled the stories she had heard of the time when Mike had been Nathan Pride's senior registrar. That they were all very friendly was obvious from the way Rowan took hold of his hand and pulled him down into the chair by her side. Not that her husband seemed to object as he looked on benevolently. Just then Rowan looked up and even at this distance Jessica could see the look they exchanged, a look which clearly said no one else existed for either of them. A wave of pure envy washed over her and it was all Jessica could do to remain in her seat.

To her dismay they were joined by Johnny Blair, one of the drug reps attending the conference. A smoothly handsome man, he was of the type which made Jessica's skin crawl. His skin was soft, white, too well cared for, his hair was too contrived, his suits that bit too tailored. He slid into the seat next to her, managing to run one hand down her arm and to press her knee with one of his as he did so. Most people treated Johnny as something of a harmless joke, but Jessica found it difficult to do so. She knew one or two women had made complaints against him, but it hadn't had any effect on his behaviour. It amazed her that the women who had to work with him coped as well as they did. The fact that he came on to so many women, chatting them up so blatantly, was used to excuse his behaviour. It couldn't really be harassment, could it, if it wasn't personal, individual? It was just the way he was.

To Jessica it could, but she knew that if she made a fuss she would be labelled the one with a problem. Johnny would just laugh and ask if she couldn't take a joke. If, when they were alone, he might mutter something about her being frigid, that was something he would make sure no one else heard. And Jessica certainly wasn't going to tell anyone.

Now Johnny was leaning over her, his body far too close for comfort, beginning a litany of her charms. Jessica didn't even bother to suppress a shudder. How was she going to get out of this? If only Mike had joined them. She would have felt very much less intimidated with his comforting bulk close by.

A strong hand took her elbow and warm breath caressed the back of her neck. Her hand trembled at the touch and drops of dry sherry were scattered across the hotel terrace. And Mike's feet. Not that he appeared to notice. 'Coming into dinner?'

There was no need to reply because Mike had taken her assent for granted and was even now propelling her across the terrace, where they had been having sherry to the door of the private dining-room.

'You looked as if you needed rescuing,' his voice whispered huskily in her ear. 'Was I right?'

Nodding vigorously, Jessica didn't trust herself to speak.

'What's the matter, Jessie?' Mike looked at her with the air of a man who knew he had missed something important, but didn't know what. 'You don't take Johnny Blair seriously, do you? He doesn't mean anything by it.'

'Maybe not, but *you* don't have to put up with him pawing you and making suggestive comments all the time.' There was more emotion in her voice that she had intended and it wasn't lost on Mike. Giving her a quick, assessing glance, then turning back to focus on the drug rep, now with his arm around the waist of a young registrar, Mike's uneven brows drew together in a lopsided scowl of true ferocity.

'I didn't realise that it would upset you so much,' he murmured slowly. 'Maybe I should. . .' He turned as though to go back and confront the other man, but Jessica caught at his arm.

'No, don't.'

'I'd have thought you'd be happy for somebody to put him straight.' Mike looked thoroughly confused.

'Yes, but not now. Not like this.'

The very real anger in Mike's face had thrown Jessica into a mild panic. Nor had she missed the way his hand had clenched in a fist at his side. The last thing she needed was for Mike to get into an altercation—no matter how minor, no matter if it was only verbal— because of her. Both their reputations would suffer and he would think even less of her. Inevitably he would end up blaming her for the whole incident.

Now that she came to think about it she was surprised he was prepared to get involved at all. Especially when she remembered what Val had told her. If he thought Johnny Blair was so harmless, why hadn't he simply ignored it?

In a daze she allowed herself to be seated at one of the circular tables with Mike firmly at her side. A second later Nathan Pride was taking the seat at her other side, his wife next to him. A covert look passed between the two men and Jessica had the uneasy feeling that Mike had planned not just this, but something else as well. What that was she couldn't fathom.

If there *were* any undercurrents Rowan acted as though she was oblivious to them, leaning forward in front of her husband to introduce herself to Jessica. 'I've been hearing all about you,' she said candidly. 'From Mike,' she added for good measure, grinning at that man, who seemed inordinately interested in his linen napkin.

From then on the evening picked up and Jessica found that she was enjoying herself more than she would have believed possible. For all that Nathan Pride could look forbidding, and had a reputation that said he sometimes took his name too literally, he put Jessica totally at her ease and set out to charm her into his legion of admirers. It was easy to fall under his spell and Jessica remembered Maggie and her soft spot for Dr Pride and her disdain for blonds. Rowan didn't appear to be in the slightest bit put out by her husband's manner, and Jessica ruefully accepted that he would behave like this to anyone, that it was nothing special about her that made him turn on the charm. She wondered how Rowan put up with it, then intercepted another of their shared glances that said the rest of the world could go hang for all they cared. Envy wasn't a pretty emotion, but Jessica knew that that was what she was feeling. She couldn't imagine ever feeling that secure about anyone. What she knew she meant was about Mike. No one else would ever enter into it.

When they moved into the bar after dinner Mike stayed close by her side, at one point his hand resting on her waist as he guided her through the throng of people. Jessica was aware of being on the receiving end of more than one knowing look, but couldn't think what to do about it. Without drawing attention to what she was doing she tried to move slightly further away from Mike but was foiled as he simply followed her. Short of her progessing backwards around the room, presumably with Mike following her, it seemed she would have to put up with the covert interest.

Surprisingly it was Nathan who rescued her, drawing her away from Mike to sit with Rowan at one of the tables, leaving Mike at the bar to get drinks for them. Again Jessica wondered if it was deliberate that he had just happened to choose a table in the corner of the room, near French windows, with a magnificent potted plant on the other side. A place where it would be difficult for anyone else to join them.

'Let's go for a walk.' Mike was sitting next to her, crowding her, on the small two-seater sofa, his breath stirring the hairs on the nape of her neck, raising goosebumps that he couldn't fail to notice.

'Now?' She whispered the word without looking at him, but knew that he had heard.

'Why not?' His breath was a caress she didn't want to stop. 'It's a beautiful night, warm, and still not quite dark.'

At this she moved slightly, her thigh brushing his as

he rested his arm along the back of the sofa, bringing their bodies closer together.

'How can we just walk out? Everybody is watching us already. What will people think?'

'That I'm very lucky.' Although Mike kept a perfectly straight face, his eyes glowed with an emotion which sent shivers of anticipation through Jessica.

No longer caring what anyone thought, Jessica rose to her feet in one gracefully fluid movement and walked through the French door without a backward glance. She gave a passing thought to what Rowan and Nathan would make of her behaviour, but instinctively knew they would understand and wouldn't judge her. She didn't need to look back to know that Mike was barely a step behind her. Leaving the terrace, they stepped into the balmy night air. Despite the warmth enveloping her like a cloak Jessica shivered again, then started with shock as Mike's arm came round her waist, steering her away from the building along the drive which would eventually lead to the sea. They were quickly out of sight of prying eyes from the hotel but, as the gravel path became more rocky, Jessica knew she wasn't going to get far.

'I should have changed my shoes. These sandals weren't made for walking.' She gazed at the strappy gold kid on her feet and sighed. They had cost a fortune and were about to be ruined.

A deep, throaty chuckle came from Mike as he pulled her off the path and into the shadows of the trees. 'I didn't really bring you out here for a hike,' he murmured as his hands circled her waist, pulling her towards him.

'Then why?'

'Because I wanted to be alone with you. Because I wanted to do this.'

Darkness descended as his head blotted out the moon, his lips claiming hers in a kiss of such gentle softness that Jessica had to open her eyes and see Mike's skin inches from her face to convince herself that it wasn't a dream. Even as she wondered the tenor of the kiss changed and Mike's lips hardened as he deepened the kiss. Large hands held her waist firmly, pulling her to him until their bodies were pressed together and he slipped his tongue between her lips, flicking across her teeth as he entered the warm moistness of her mouth.

A liquid fire spread through her and, pressing her body against his Jessica was rewarded by an increase in tension in him as his hands slipped downwards to her hips to press her tightly against him. Her breath caught in her throat as she felt his arousal. Arching her body, she moved against him and heard his intake of breath as his lips left hers to trail a fiery path along her jaw, down her neck and across the skin to which her off-the-shoulder dress gave him access. She wanted more of him, thrilling with the anticipation of feeling his hands travel over her whole body, stroking her skin to an exquisite pitch of arousal.

The sound of laughter coming from the path caused them to spring apart and Mike drew her further into the shadows. They watched in silence as a young couple, arms entwined around each other and both looking as though they had had slightly too much to drink, made their unsteady way to the beach.

Taking her hand in his, Mike pulled her back towards the path. 'Come on. Let's get away from here.'

She wasn't sure if she had consciously made a

decision or whether she just went along with the mood of the moment, with Mike's apparent assumption of what would happen, but they were in her room before she realised the choice had been made. There was still time to back out of further commitment, she told herself just as Mike's lips closed on hers. And at that precise moment any choice there might have been disappeared. As his mouth caressed her his hands were moulding her body to his, holding her so that she was left in not the slightest doubt of how much he wanted her. She buried her face in the side of his neck, breathing in the scent of him that was far more powerful than any cologne could be. His hands were sliding up her body; she felt the zip of her dress give under his gentle tugging and, as the filmy material fell away from her body to pool around her feet, it was as though her uncertainties and inhibitions fell with it. It was a revelation how small and delicate she could feel as Mike picked her up in his arms, carrying her to the bed to place her gently on the covers before lying down beside her.

She had never doubted that Mike would be an expert lover but his generosity, his consideration for her and willingness to wait for her to match him in arousal and demand, touched her in a way sheer technique did not. When he finally entered her it was because she could no longer bear not to have his possession as his body took her to places she had never imagined, never sought to explore.

Even when their passion was spent he didn't let go of her, but rolled them on to their sides, cradling her body against his as he wrapped his arms tightly around her.

'Twin beds,' he muttered sleepily against her ear.

'Why couldn't you have been given a room with a double bed?'

'Mmm.' If there was a more sensible answer Jessica couldn't think of it, instead contenting herself with wriggling against him, delighting in feeling the instant response in his body.

Their coming together was more urgent this time, but none the less satisfying for that.

Jessica was sorry when Mike whispered that he had to go back to his own room, but was too sleepy to protest. Anyway, she could see the sense in it. Neither of them would want Mike to be seen coming out of her room in the morning, and they weren't going to get much sleep in the narrow bed. Secure in the knowledge that this was only the first of a never-ending succession of nights with Mike, Jessica let him go.

She passed the next day in a daze as she could barely wait to be alone with Mike again. The journey home would give them a chance to talk, then the evening stretched before them. Jessica gave up trying to follow the complicated statistics being presented in the paper given by a very worthy but very dull senior registrar, who had much to learn about delivery, and focused on a romantic dinner, followed by another night of abandoned lovemaking with Mike. Her cheeks flamed. Mike, sitting next to her, noticed and winked, which only served to enhance her colour. Surely he wasn't telepathic?

She was lying in his arms in the warm afterglow of love when the blow fell. And it all started so unthinkingly.

'I didn't know it could be like this.' She pressed her body along the length of his, her hands moving across his chest as her fingers threaded through the downy mat of blond hair.

Mike gathered her close, holding her tighter at those words, but said nothing. He hadn't yet told her he loved her and, although Jessica's heart insisted that he must, her head was telling her it was by no means a sure thing. Letting her hand begin to trail slowly down his body, Jessica was satisfied to hear him catch his breath and feel his stomach muscles clench with tension and expectation.

Soft laughter gurgled from her. 'I'm not quite such a helpless female, after all, hmm?'

A brief grunt of laughter from Mike told her she had scored a point, only to lose it instantly as he captured both her hands in his, rolling her over on to her back and pinning her beneath him as his lips sought hers.

'What was that you were saying about not being helpless?' he asked conversationally, while his lips traced a path down her throat to her breast which made her catch her breath and gasp in her turn.

Quite content to stay where she was, she made a half-hearted attempt to move from underneath him, but Mike held her there effortlessly, his blue eyes darkening to navy as he watched her.

'I didn't think you approved of helpless woman,' she murmured, stilling her languid attempts to free herself.

'I don't,' he confirmed, and to Jessica's consternation rolled away from her, although one arm still rested heavily across her waist. He was distancing himself from her psychologically, she could tell, and the loss of emotional warmth was more chilling than the loss of the physical comfort of his body wrapped round hers.

'Tell me about it,' she whispered, her breath fanning his cheek, and was later to wish those words unsaid.

Moving on to his back to stare at the ceiling, carefully not touching her, he began to speak. Mike, it turned out, was the youngest of three brothers, the oldest being Jake's father. All three had taken after their father, a rural GP, in size and temperament. Their mother had been a tiny, delicate, doll-like woman who had relied heavily on her husband. She had hated rural life and the lack of sophisticated amenities which came of living in the wilds of Scotland and had taken off for the bright lights with a visitor from London who had been on holiday.

'Leaving her sons?' Jessica was scandalised.

'Leaving her sons,' Mike confirmed. 'I was seven. My father took it hard. He had been devoted to her and from then on he turned against women—all women—but particularly helpless females, as he called them. I remember him telling me not to trust helpless women all my life.'

Her heart running cold, Jessica heard Jake's voice echoing the same words. Words he'd said Mike had passed on to him.

'My two brothers were both quite a bit older and it wasn't long before they went off to university in turn. Neither came back to live while I was still at home. Forbes, Jake's father, met and married Caroline and stayed in Glasgow. He's been lucky. But not Kav.'

'Kav?' Jessica was lost.

'Kavan. My other brother. He followed our father into general practice and took over when Dad retired. His wife, a helpless, useless type if ever there was one, and totally selfish, left Kav a few weeks before Christmas. Kav was very cut up about it. I was coming back from seeing him when we met in the blizzard.'

Her mind flew back to that meeting. She had never

known why he had been on the road. He had been returning from offering comfort and support to his brother. No wonder he had been so dismissive of helpless women!

'But not all women are like that,' Jessica protested, all the while a chill taking hold of her heart, spreading ice along her viens. Mike couldn't really be that blinkered, could he? It seemed he could.

'I enjoy being with you,' he told her, still not touching her. 'I more than enjoy making love with you, but. . .' His voice trailed away, leaving Jessica uncertain as to whether he didn't know what he wanted to say, or whether he did know but couldn't bring himself to put it into words. So she said it for him.

'But you don't want anything permanent. That *is* what you are trying to say, isn't it, Mike?'

He moved restlessly and rolled to face her, but when he would have captured one of her hands she withdrew them.

'I guess it is. I. . .I'm very fond of you, Jessie, but——' He stopped suddenly to raise himself on to one elbow and look down at her. 'We can have a good time together, you'll see,' he stated confidently, but she could see the hesitation in his eyes.

And that was when she lost her temper. 'You're nothing but a coward, you know that? An emotional coward! This is all just some excuse because you're too scared to commit yourself to anyone. You don't want anyone making demands on you, so you make sure no one can get close to you. You're——'

'That's not true!' Mike's face and voice both betrayed his total confusion at her attack, but Jessica wasn't to be silenced.

In the end they both said things which in the cold

light of day they wished they hadn't, but by then it was too late. Mike took himself off, all injured dignity, and Jessica was left trying to convince herself she had never loved Mike—and failing dismally.

CHAPTER TEN

'DID you or did you not say that men shouldn't become psychiatrists?'

How had it come to this? Mike was scowling at her, his dark, oddly matched brows pulled together in a truly ferocious frown, meeting above his handsome nose in an almost straight line. Never had he looked so much like a Viking warrior intent on rape and pillage. Scratch the last bit, Jessica, she told herself. But destruction was certainly on his mind.

Stuart, on the other hand, was having trouble not smiling. Looking decidedly smug, he was standing back from the other two, hands thrust negligently in his pockets as his eyes darted from one to the other.

Not willing to be seen going down without a fight, Jessica metaphorically and literally squared her shoulders and launched an attack of her own. She confessed.

'Yes, I did. At the time I meant it, and in the same circumstances I would probably say the same thing. I didn't think Stuart had heard. I'm not sure why he was eavesdropping on a conversation I was having with someone else, and I certainly don't know why he has raised it now.'

She met Mike's brooding gaze with the light of battle in her eyes, something which seemed to disconcert him, for he looked away, first at the floor and then, with a sudden intensity, at Stuart.

'Stuart seems to think that you are somehow conspiring with the other staff to undermine his authority.'

'Exactly how am I supposed to have done this?'

Mike's eyes never left Stuart's face. 'You wanted this out in the open,' he told the younger man. 'I suggest you substantiate your accusation now and we try to get to the bottom of it, then lay it to rest.'

'I'm not sure. . .' Stuart hesitated, and Jessica got the impression that he hadn't expected to be put on the spot like this.

'As though we haven't got enough on our hands. . .' Mike muttered half under his breath, leaving Jessica to assume he was talking to himself and wasn't expecting any sort of reply. 'I haven't got time to mess about with petty bickering between you two,' he flung at Stuart, and Jessica breathed an inward sigh of relief. He wasn't going to take Stuart's poisoned barbs seriously. Her heart sank as he continued, 'But neither do I intend to let this situation get out of hand. If you've got something to say, say it.'

It turned out that Stuart did have something to say, but none of it was very sensible, and none of it could be called a real accusation or challenge to her behaviour. It was more a litany of imagined slights and misrepresented half-truths. When it became obvious that Stuart didn't have concrete examples of behaviour to cite as flouting his authority, Mike's already precarious temper threatened to get out of control altogether.

'You've made a serious accusation against Dr Balfour,' he pointed out to Stuart firmly, cutting him off in mid-flow, 'and appear to have nothing with which to substantiate your claim. I think we should let the matter drop.'

Stuart looked slightly abashed, but that wasn't

enough for Jessica. She had been accused, as she saw it, of unprofessional behaviour and she didn't see why Stuart should be allowed to get away with it.

'I'm not sure that I want to let it drop,' she announced, causing both men to turn on her with similar expressions of shock. It was almost as though they had forgotten that she was there, was an active rather than a passive participant in the situation.

'Jessica——'

'If you want a——'

Both men spoke but, at a warning glance from Mike, Stuart fell silent.

'I'm suggesting you drop this,' Mike elaborated, 'because, as far as I can see, and as my old granny would say, "It's six of one and half a dozen of the other". Stuart, I think you should apologise to Dr Balfour, but I would also ask you, Jessica, to look to your behaviour and your attitudes. The female solidarity thing can get a bit heavy in here at times and the others tend to look to you for leadership on that kind of thing. A bit more give and take, not to mention old-fashioned tolerance, wouldn't come amiss.'

'How dare——?'

'Jessica!' Mike cut her off sharply before she could say anything more. 'I wouldn't if I were you. So far nothing has been said that need go any further than this room. I assume you'd both rather keep it that way.'

'Yes, sir.' By the look on his face, Stuart was beginning to realise that accusing Jessica without having anything to back it up hadn't been the smartest move. Now his only concern was to get out of the room and hope the incident would be forgotten. By Michael Knight, at least.

'Jessica?' Mike's tone indicated that not only was he waiting for an acknowledgement from her, but that he wasn't about to take any nonsense. She had better agree, or else.

'Yes.' She knew her tone was sulky, but didn't much care. Stuart might not have had anything concrete to say but he had still managed to get Mike on his side. And it was that which really hurt. Not that Stuart was behaving like a wee boy who couldn't get his own way, but that Mike really seemed to believe that there was something in his allegations, even if it couldn't be proven.

The glance Mike flicked at Stuart so clearly indicated dismissal that the registrar nearly fell over his own feet in his haste to leave the room. As the door closed behind him the tension increased dramatically and Jessica knew she couldn't take any more. Turning, she too almost ran for the door.

'Jessica.' Mike's voice urged her to wait, but she couldn't face him again. Her hand was on the handle but he tried again. 'Jessica! Wait!' But with a sob she had wrenched the door open and was running down the corridor as though her life depended on it.

She made it to her car before she realised that she couldn't just walk out on her commitments and responsibilities to her patients. But she couldn't just meekly walk back in either. An early lunch was called for.

It was only as she was drinking her second cup of coffee in a local café that she realised that although Mike had suggested that Stuart should apologise to her for his insinuations he had not done so. And she didn't think it likely that he would, or that Mike would insist, even if he remembered.

She was left wondering how much longer she could

stay in her current job. If only she could hold out until Val came back she would be all right. And short of walking out totally, and ruining her career, there wasn't much else she could do. Handing in her notice and looking for another job would take far too long. The only thing left was to tackle Mike. The tension between them was noticeable and was affecting everyone else, and that really couldn't be allowed to continue.

'I thought I'd find you here.' Mike pulled out a chair and slid into the space opposite her. 'Do you want to explain?'

'Explain!' The word exploded from her as she was filled with a sense of righteous indignation. It wasn't up to her to explain anything. But as quickly as her temper had risen the fight went out of her and she shrugged. 'What's to explain? Stuart and I don't see eye to eye over the treatment of some patients. There's nothing very exciting in that.'

'I wasn't talking about Stuart, as well you know,' Mike ground out through clenched teeth. 'I was asking why you saw fit to run out of my office without waiting to hear what I had to say.'

Jessica shrugged again. It was getting to be a habit. 'Because I didn't want to hear you make excuses for Stuart. I didn't want to hear you say that you thought the situation was my fault. I didn't want to hear you defend the indefensible. I——'

Mike butted in, holding his hand up in front of him in mock-surrender, 'OK, OK I get the picture.' The laughter threaded through his voice and it was the sound of that which stirred the remnants of her temper.

'No, you don't. That's the point. You don't understand anything.'

'I understand that you're being overly emotional about this. We have to work together and——'

'Not if I leave, we don't.' Where had the words come from? That wasn't what she had intended to say, but it was almost worth it to see the look of comic surprise on Mike's face. He obviously hadn't expected her to say anything like that either.

'You can't mean that.' The words were whispered hoarsely, as though the breath had been knocked out of him.

'I can.'

'It would ruin your career. You. . .' His voice trailed away and Jessica took delight in the fact that she had, for once, silenced him. Silenced and shocked him. The colour had drained from his face, leaving it curiously ashen.

'I know. That's the only thing that's keeping me here right now. My career is more important to me than anything else and I don't see why I should let you, or some wee lad, drive me into something I'll regret.'

Mike's breathing seemed to ease a little at that, and some of the colour returned to his cheeks. 'We can't go on like this,' he told her firmly, as though coming to a decision. 'Have dinner with me tonight and we'll find a way out of this mess.' He reached across the table and gently stroked her cheek, tucking a stray wisp of hair behind her ear. 'There *has* to be a way out of this. I don't want to lose you, Jessie.' For such large, strong-looking hands they could be infinitely gentle. The words were more a plea than a statement, and that was enough to lift Jessica's spirits and allow her to suggest that they had both deserted the hospital long enough and maybe they should return to their respective duties. They could talk later.

She followed him in her car, staying close behind his Volvo. Ever after she would remember the accident as though it had happened in slow motion, although at the time it was over in a few seconds. A red car with two young boys in it shot out of a side-road with no warning and straight into the side of Mike's car with such speed and force that Mike's bigger car was still thrust sideways and Jessica watched with horror as he struggled to control it. But it was too late. As the car went into a skid the lorry coming in the other direction slowed, but not fast enough. Mike's car bounced off the front of the oncoming lorry, slewed round, skidded across the road and went bonnet-first into a lamp-post. Jessica had already stopped as the screech of tortured metal followed by the almighty thud of impact reached her. She was out of the car and running towards Mike before she had time to think. All traffic had come to a standstill, not helped by her car abandoned on the other side of the road. Despite the bonnet being crumpled to half its size against the lamp-post, Jessica could hear that the engine was still running, then realised that the ominous smell of petrol filled the air. It could only come from a leak in Mike's car. Of him there was no sign. He hadn't got out and now Jessica could see him slumped over the wheel, unmoving.

'Oh, God, no! No!' She wasn't aware that she had screamed the words as she dashed distractedly towards the car.

A man caught at her arm as she rushed past him. 'You can't go there, hen. It could explode at any minute.'

She didn't even look at him as she wrenched her arm free and continued relentlessly forward. The smell of petrol was worse, but she closed her mind to anything but getting to Mike, getting him out of the car.

Reaching it, she tugged at the door, but it wouldn't open. Without hesitation she pulled open the back door and climbed in, crawling over the seat to reach Mike in the front. There was blood everywhere, streaming from cuts across his forehead where the windscreen had shattered, but she could hear the hoarse sound of his breath as it rattled in his chest. The dashboard was smashed and crumpled and at first Jessica thought Mike was pinned under the steering-wheel, but a quick survey showed that it was his seatbelt which was holding him in place. There wasn't room to do much more that a hasty examination, and as she ran her hands over him Jessica willed back every scrap of knowledge that she could remember about trauma injuries. From what she could feel, Mike was in one piece. She was worried about his continued unconsciousness but even as her mind was ticking off possibilities he groaned, but did not move.

The smell of leaking petrol had had the effect of keeping people well back, although Jessica could see an ever-growing circle of bystanders at a distance. She hoped to God that someone had phoned for an ambulance and the fire brigade. But getting through the busy city traffic could take a while. Getting Mike out of the car before they both went up in flames was the priority. Even if he did have other injuries that she hadn't detected, it was better than being blown apart.

Unlocking his seat belt, she pushed him back from his slumped position over the steering-wheel and was relieved to see that, despite the copious amounts of blood, his face wasn't badly damaged. Most of the injuries looked to be fairly minor. He had been unbelievably lucky.

Lucky! She would have laughed if she had had time. When she had got them both out of there, that would be the time to start thinking about being lucky.

There was no way she could pull Mike over the seat. The door might be buckled, but somehow she was going to have to get it open. She reached across to release the catch and at that moment realised that there was someone on the other side of the door. A body in dark blue bent down and peered through the window and Jessica found herself looking into the eyes of a very young, very anxious-looking policeman. He looked like a baby!

Now is not the time to start worrying about how young the police are looking, she told herself firmly and, giving him a fleeting grin and a thumbs-up sign, indicated the door handle, miming that he should try to pull the door open from his side. Immediately understanding what she wanted, he applied his considerable youthful energy and strength to tugging on the door. Deciding that she could risk lying across Mike, Jessica shifted position so that she could kick at the door with her feet. With a suddenness that caused both her and the young policeman to lose their balance the door gave way, with a screech of twisted metal as it fell open.

Without wasting a second Jessica had moved off Mike and was pushing him through the door as the policemen reached in to help lift him out. Fortunately he was brawny, despite his youth, and, getting a arm around Mike and under his arms, was able to drag his torso from the car as Jessica dealt with freeing Mike's feet and pushing him out. She took back everything she had thought about baby-faced policeman. This one was worth his not inconsiderable bulk in gold. He had saved precious minutes in getting Mike out of the car, and Jessica acknowledged the difficulties she would have had in trying to manipulate Mike's massive frame on her own. Almost falling out of the car, she joined the policeman in his hold under Mike's arms and together they dragged him away from the car just as the wail of the ambulance siren sounded a few streets away, to be instantly followed by the sound of the fire brigade approaching from the opposite direction. Another constable was urging the crowd of spectators back as they had surged forward when Mike had first emerged from the car.

'Keep them back,' Jessica heard 'her' policeman shout just as she saw two more emerge from a squad car and start directing everyone further away from the damaged car. By now sobbing with relief, Jessica was beyond thinking of anything but that they were safe, and was in no mood to object when one of the policemen raced forward and knocked her out of the way to take hold of Mike's legs as the two men carried him to safety.

And not before time. With a mighty roar the leaking petrol finally ignited and the car exploded in an inferno of leaping flames.

The noise and the blast almost knocked Jessica off her feet, but the heat of the flames at her back pushed her onward, her concentration totally on Mike, not looking back to see what had happened.

The next few minutes were a blur of confused shapes and images. Yellow-helmeted men ran past, taking no notice of her as she sank to the ground in a welter of shock and exhaustion. She was barely aware of being led to the ambulance, only starting to protest as she was urged to enter. It was the sight of Mike strapped to a stretcher inside that pushed her forward and she clambered in with all haste, determined that he should get to the hospital as soon as possible.

She heard an ambulance siren sounding somewhere close to hand and realised with a sense of horror that it was for them. By the time they pulled into the casualty forecourt she was shivering uncontrollably and her teeth were chattering with shock as tears rolled down her cheeks. Now the full horror of the accident was coming home to her, and she found her mind concentrating on 'what if?' as her imagination played over and over again, in slow motion and glorious Technicolour, not just what *had* happened, but what *might* have happened. When a junior nurse led her away to the privacy of a curtained cubicle she was content to sit and sob quietly until someone came to deal with her.

Standing outside the door of the private room where Mike had been put, Jessica smoothed down her skirt and took several deep breaths. It didn't help. Her heart was still pounding like an overworked drill and her breathing was noticeably shallow. Not that she thought Mike would be up to noticing very much. He had been unbelievably lucky, his only injuries being minor cuts and bruises to his head, a mild concussion and major bruising across his chest where the seat belt had held him as he had been thrown against it on impact.

After a thorough check-up Jessica had been allowed to go home. Told to go home, in fact, as she had insisted on waiting to find out what had happened to Mike. Naomi had arrived and dragged her away, saying that a bath, a change of clothes and some non-institutional tea would do her the world of good and she could still get back before they had finished all their X-raying of Mike.

The talk of X-rays and concussion had reminded her of the evening he had fallen down the stairs, and for some unaccountable reason that had set the tears off again. He had blamed her for that. Maybe he would blame her for this. Everything always seemed to be her fault. Maybe it *was* her fault. If she hadn't run out of the hospital in the first place he wouldn't have had to come after her, and he wouldn't have been on the road to be in the way of the youthful joyriders.

Joyriders. A misnomer if ever there was one. She wondered what had happened to them, if they were all right, or if they too had been hurt. Part of her wanted to hope that they had been, that they too were suffering, but she couldn't sustain the emotion. It all seemed so pointless. As long as Mike was going to be all right, nothing else really mattered.

She had been reassured on that point by the A and E consultant, but knew that until she had seen him for herself she wouldn't fully believe it. So why was she standing outside his door, her heart hammering like a pneumatic drill, frightened to open it and go in? Telling herself that if she could get into the car at the accident she could certainly go into his private room, she steeled herself and opened the door.

Apart from looking a decidedly pale shade of grey, against which the bruises stood out with frightening intensity, Mike looked much as usual—big, handsome, the cuts and bruises giving him a very rakish air as though he were being restrained against his will. So intent was she on his face that it was a second before she noticed that his chest was bare. When she did, all she could do was stare—at the skin rippling over tightly coiled muscles, at the blond hair which spread across its width to arrow down to be hidden by the sheet tucked firmly round his waist, and at the dark band of bruising which ran diagonally across his chest—evidence that the seat belt had saved him from a very much worse fate. A slight movement caught Jessica's eye and she realised that he wasn't quite as at ease as he would have had her believe, for one hand was nervously—probably unconsciously—pleating then smoothing the blanket that covered him.

Her voice felt locked in her throat, her mouth and lips dry and numb, and no sound came. Mike looked to be in a similar condition. She could almost hear the seconds tick past before she found the ability to speak.

'How do you feel?' Not exactly original, but she was inordinately pleased that she had been able to say anything at all.

'I'll live.' Mike cracked a smile, then winced, as though the movement hurt him. 'Once I get rid of this headache.'

She nodded, knowing in that instant that if she tried to speak she would only cry. The silence stretched again.

'How are you? No ill-effects?' The words sounded as though Mike too was having to force them out, that he was damping down some flood of emotion, and Jessica felt the guilt come up to swamp her once again. How could she possibly atone for all the trouble she had caused him? Simply saying she was sorry wasn't nearly enough. But it would have to do for a start.

'I'm fine.' The words eased her back into speech. 'Mike, I'm so——'

'Jessica, I don't know——'

They spoke together and stopped together, exchanging the sheepish smiles of people who were ill at ease with one another. We could be strangers, Jessica thought with panic, but didn't know how to make the situation easier. An apology would only remind them both that it was her fault that he was there, lying in a hospital bed, lucky to be alive.

'You were saying. . .?' She looked vaguely in his direction, totally unable to meet his eyes. She was frightened by what she might read in their compelling blue depths—blame, condemnation?

He looked even more uncomfortable at that. 'No. You finish what you were saying.'

She took a steadying breath. It was now or never. 'I'm so sorry.' Her voice caught on the ever-increasing lump in her throat. Then the words were tumbling out of her with a speed that all but made them incomprehensible. 'Oh, Mike, it's all my fault. I'm so sorry. You could have been killed. I'll never forgive myself. If anything had happened to you. . .' The tears that had been threatening for so long overcame her control and coursed down her cheeks, misting her vision, but not enough so that she couldn't see the total incomprehension on Mike's stunned face.

'What are you talking about, woman?' Mike moved in the bed as though he would get up but he was obviously in no condition to be making sudden movements because he fell back against the pillows with a low groan.

Jessica did not move but stood silently, tears still overflowing her eyes, but making no sound. Mike held out his hand to her. 'Jessica. Come here.' Like a child obeying instructions from a parent, Jessica moved forward without conscious volition until Mike could catch hold of her hand and pull her down on the bed beside him. 'Let's start again. What on earth are you talking about? What have you got to be sorry about?'

Although she had managed to get some control over the shaming tears, it was her heart-rate, not to mention her breathing, which was now causing her some concern. Mike hadn't let go of her hand after he had pulled her down to the bed, and now his thumb was running over the back of it, moving down to massage the inner side of her wrist, where he must surely be able to feel the racing of her pulse.

'The accident. It's all my fault. I——'

He cut her off incredulously. 'Your fault! How in God's name could it possibly be your fault? It was a couple of kids in a stolen car. What on earth has that got to do with you?' By now he sounded, to Jessica's anxious ears, not only disbelieving but impatient as well. Was she never going to do anything right?

'It was my fault you were there. If I hadn't gone rushing off like that you wouldn't have come after me and——'

'And if I hadn't been such an idiot you wouldn't have had to go dashing off in the first place. If anything, the fault is mine.'

'No! I should have——' He placed gentle fingers against her lips, silencing her, a tender smile playing around his lips.

'Shh! We could sit here arguing about whose fault it is for hours, when the truth is it was nothing to do with either of us. It was an accident. If the blame lies with anyone it's with the joyriding kids. They've both got minor injuries and are recovering along the corridor, I understand, under the watchful eye of a very annoyed policeman, two furious fathers and two mothers ready to kill them. If I were them, I think I'd go into police custody quietly and quickly. But we won't think about them now.' His hold on her hand tightened.

'It's my turn now. Words are inadequate to thank you for what you did. It's not enough to say you saved my life—thank you. It was so much more than that. It wasn't just that you saved me, but that you put your own life at risk to do so.' He shuddered. 'When I think of what could have happened——'

'But it didn't.' It was Jessica's turn to reassure him now.

'But——' He cut himself off. 'No. You're right. There's no point in dwelling on what *might* have happened. I'll always be in your debt, Jessica. There's no way I'll ever be able to repay you properly.'

Loving me would be a start, Jessica thought, but of course she didn't say so. And then she realised how impossible it would be now. If Mike said anything to her, if he suggested resuming any kind of relationship, she would always wonder if he was doing it out of a sense of gratitude, of obligation. The thought tore at her heart and it was all she could do to prevent a moan escaping her lips. Something of what she felt must have shown on her face, for Mike frowned, catching her other hand and holding both of them in one of his massive ones, while the other slowly stroked the hair away from her face, his eyes boring into hers.

'What is it? Why that look? What are you thinking of?'

'It's nothing.' Her voice was surprisingly steady, showing none of the torrent of emotion tearing her apart. All she wanted to do was get out of there.

'Ah, Jessie.' That Mike didn't believe her was obvious. In one swift movement he had gathered her close, holding her tight against his battered chest, never noticing the discomfort as he gently rocked her in his arms, muttering incoherent words of comfort.

Jessica gave herself up to the bliss of being in his arms, burying her face against his neck, feeling the sensual comfort of his chin rubbing against her cheek.

'Jessie, I've been such a fool. I love you so much. I don't think I realised how much until I saw that lamp-post heading towards me and I thought that I might die without ever having told you. That was the worst moment. Knowing that you would never know.' His arms tightened as he paused, as though expecting some response, but there was nothing Jessica could say.

With each word she had felt the ice form round her heart, protecting herself from believing his words. She wanted to believe them too much. But she couldn't take the knowledge that it was his gratitude speaking. Or that he knew how she felt and pitied her. That was almost worse.

'Jessie?' He sounded hesitant but still she could not say anything, could not move. It was too much like heaven being held by him, breathing in the scent of him, feeling his warm skin against her fingers, through the thin cotton of her dress, feeling the movement of his lips against her neck. 'Jessie, do you think that's selfish of me?' His voice broke the spell and she wriggled in his grasp, trying to free herself from the embrace she didn't want to leave. For an instant she didn't think he was going to let her go, then his arms loosened and fell to his sides and she was able to sit up. One quick look at his face told her that she couldn't meet his eyes and she let her gaze drop, missing the pain that clouded his before it was replaced by a more speculative glint.

'Of course it wouldn't really matter unless you loved me too, would it?' If he had hoped that that would shock her into looking at him he was disappointed for Jessica kept her eyes downcast, fixed on her hands grasped tightly together in her lap.

'Did you know that some cultures believe that if you save a person's life you own that life?' His tone was conversational, as though he were discussing something of no great moment, and Jessica risked a quick glance at him. His bland expression was not as reassuring as it should have been. He was playing some new game with her and Jessica didn't know what the rules were. 'How do you feel about owning me, Jessica?'

She couldn't sit there silently forever; she would have to answer some time. 'Don't be silly.' The words came out on a croak. 'You don't owe me anything at all.'

'And if I think I do?'

She shrugged. 'I'm just glad you're alive. Can't we leave it at that?'

Mike sighed, somewhat theatrically, Jessica thought. 'At least you didn't say, I'd have done the same for anyone. I'm not sure I would have believed that, anyway.' He was beginning to sound insufferably smug to Jessica's ear and she just wanted to get out of the private room, away from him and his probing of her guilty secret.

'Can't we just forget it?' By now Jessica was beginning to sound slightly desperate, which was as nothing compared to what she was feeling.

'Are you sure that's what you want?' Was there some hidden purpose in Mike's words? After the gently bantering tone he had been using his voice had switched to sounding totally serious. Jessica didn't have the time or emotional energy to think about it.

'Yes.'

'So I don't owe you anything?'

'No.'

'You're wrong there. I do owe you something. I owe you an apology.'

Jessica sneaked another quick glance at him. What trick was he playing now? 'For what?' Against her better judgement she would go along with it.

'I've misjudged you. All along. Maybe it was the way we met. And the family problems I was dealing with at the time.' His lips twisted in a wry grin. 'But, whatever it was, I wrote you off as a helpless female, someone who relied on others to get her out of the messes she got into. I saw you as someone who depended on others, who would expect to be rescued, protected, to have everything done for her.'

'But——'

Mike cut her off. 'I know you're not like that. Despite all the minor scrapes you seem to get yourself into, I know you're nothing like...my mother. Or my sister-in-law, come to that. I was blaming you for their faults. Or what I saw as faults. Maybe I was looking at things in the wrong way.'

A slow anger began to burn inside Jessica. How dared he? How dared he condemn her for the sins of other women? How dared he be so condemning in the first place? And now how dared he apologise when what he was really doing was forgiving her when she had proved herself by saving his life? How dared he be so patronising? This time she did look up and meet his eyes. The glint in his was more than matched by the fire burning in hers.

'Well, that's big of you. I'm not sure that I want your apology. You've condemned me for being something I'm not. You've judged me and—'

'Marry me, Jessica.'

That stopped her in mid-flow and she didn't know whether to laugh or cry. This was what she had wanted to hear him say. This was what she wanted above all else. Only now it was too late. She couldn't possibly marry him now.

Mike had smiled as he'd said it, but now his face was completely serious. 'I know what you think, Jessica. That it's out of gratitude. It's not. There will never be an easy time to ask you to marry me, now. The fact that you saved my life has seen to that. You'll always suspect my motives. But I do love you. You're clever and brave and funny and independent and, it has to be said, occasionally clumsy and prone to getting yourself into. . .shall we say, peculiar situations? But that doesn't alter the fact that I love you, that I've probably loved you from the moment I first saw you, and I want to marry you.'

Jessica shook her head, trying to be strong, trying not to fling herself at him and say she'd marry him, that she would take him on any terms. 'It wouldn't work, Mike,' she told him, unable actually to force the word no through her lips.

She knew she had done the right thing when Mike didn't look particularly put out at her words, merely shrugging, then cutting in to her heart as he said, 'If you're sure.'

'Yes, I'm sure. It's just gratitude and that you don't think I'm quite as hopeless as you did. It's a nice thought, but—' She stopped just in time to prevent her voice from breaking. 'I'd better go now.'

Mike made no move to stop her and the few steps to the door were the hardest she had ever taken.

'If you're going then maybe you'd better have this.'

She turned and saw that Mike had something in his hand, but she couldn't see what.

'What is it?' She took a step forward.

'Come and get it.'

She couldn't see what he was holding, but nevertheless moved back to the side of the bed.

'I bought it for you. I would still like you to have it. I shall never want to give it to anyone else.'

Jessica held out her hand, not quite looking at what Mike held, and was confused by the weight of a small square box being placed into her palm. She did look then, and felt her heart trip before beginning to beat faster than before. It looked like...but it couldn't be...could it?

'Aren't you going to open it?'

Her fingers wouldn't move; there was nothing she wanted more than to open the small box, but the power to do it wasn't there. Mike took the box from her and flicked the lid open so that Jessica could see the most perfect square-cut diamond ring winking at her from its bed of black velvet. He reached for her hand. 'Let me put it on for you.'

In a daze she watched him push the ring on to the third finger of her left hand where it fitted perfectly. She raised big round eyes, glistening with unshed tears, to his. 'I don't understand. I...'

'I bought it the day after the conference. The day after we spent the night together and had that stupid, terrible fight. I knew then that I would marry you. That I didn't want to go through life without you. But I was scared.'

'Scared?'

'I kept remembering my mother. And Kavan's wife. I knew you weren't like that. I knew you were all the things I wanted. I knew that I loved you. But it was difficult for me to admit it. God knows why. I'm sorry I put you through the things I did. I can't undo the past, but I can do everything I can to make it up to you in the future.' He grinned the slow grin that broke through his autocratic expression like the sun emerging from behind some rather dark clouds. 'What do you say?'

Jessica just kept looking at the ring on her finger. It looked so right there. But she couldn't speak.

'Say yes, Jessica.'

She wanted to, but something held her back.

'Say yes, Jessica.'

'I've always loved you,' she heard herself say, and wondered why she had felt the need to say that.

'Of course you have.' Mike spoke as though it was inconceivable that she should have done otherwise. 'Say yes.'

'And it is true that I'm slightly—only slightly, mind you—prone to getting into mildly unfortunate situations and that you'll have to keep bailing me out of messes.'

'That's what knights are for. Say yes, Jessica.'

'And I want a career, to be a consultant and——'

'Of course you do. Anyway, we'll need your salary.'

'What?'

'Children can be very expensive. And I think we should have several. Say yes, Jessica.'

'Are you really, really sure?' She met his eyes as she asked the question and the look in them was all she needed as an answer.

With a sob of relief she flung herself into his arms, quite forgetful of his injured chest, but Mike, with knightly fortitude, simply gathered her close, covering her lips with his in a kiss that went on and on. As she gave herself up to the glory of his kisses she heard him muttering something in her ear.

'Say yes, Jessica.'

Finally she capitulated.

'Yes, Jessica.'

10th anniversary
Temptation is Ten!

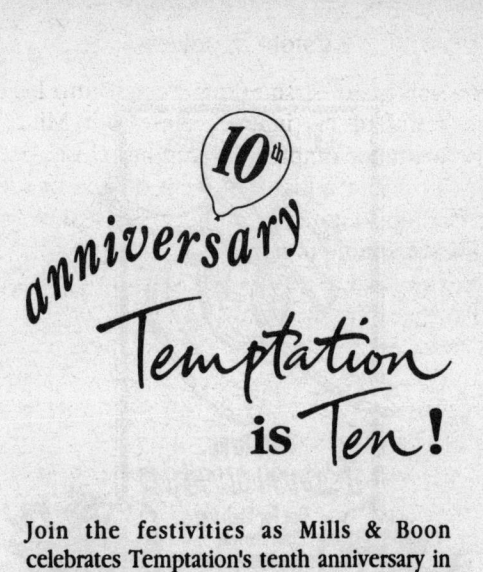

Join the festivities as Mills & Boon celebrates Temptation's tenth anniversary in February 1995.

There's a whole host of in-book competitions and special offers with some great prizes to be won—watch this space for more details!

In March, we have a sizzling new mini-series Lost Loves about love lost...love found. And, of course, the Temptation range continues to offer you fun, sensual exciting stories all year round.

After ten tempting years, nobody can resist

Temptation 10th anniversary

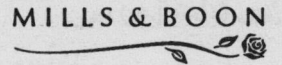

MILLS & BOON

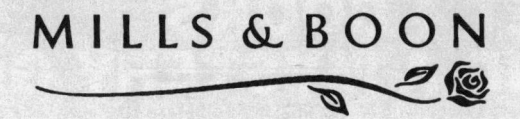

LOVE ON CALL

The books for enjoyment this month are:

STORM HAVEN Marion Lennox
IN AT THE DEEP END Laura MacDonald
NO LONGER A STRANGER Margaret O'Neill
KNIGHT'S MOVE Flora Sinclair

♥ ♥ ♥ ♥ ♥

Treats in store!

Watch next month for the following absorbing stories:

ANYONE CAN DREAM Caroline Anderson
SECRETS TO KEEP Josie Metcalfe
UNRULY HEART Meredith Webber
CASUALTY OF PASSION Sharon Wirdnam

Available from W.H. Smith, John Menzies, Volume One, Forbuoys, Martins, Tesco, Asda, Safeway and other paperback stockists.

Also available from Mills & Boon Reader Service, Freepost, P.O. Box 236, Croydon, Surrey CR9 9EL.

Readers in South Africa - write to:
IBS, Private Bag X3010, Randburg 2125.

GET 4 BOOKS AND A MYSTERY GIFT

FREE

Return the coupon below and we'll send you 4 Love on Call novels absolutely FREE! We'll even pay the postage and packing for you.

We're making you this offer to introduce you to the benefits of Reader Service: FREE home delivery of brand-new Love on Call novels, at least a month before they are available in the shops, FREE gifts and a monthly Newsletter packed with information.

Accepting these FREE books places you under no obligation to buy, you may cancel at any time, even after receiving just your free shipment. Simply complete the coupon below and send it to:

HARLEQUIN MILLS & BOON, **FREEPOST**, PO BOX 70, CROYDON CR9 9EL.

Yes, please send me 4 Love on Call novels and a mystery gift as explained above. Please also reserve a subscription for me. If I decide to subscribe I shall receive 4 superb new titles every month for just £7.20* postage and packing free. I understand that I am under no obligation whatsoever. I may cancel or suspend my subscription at any time simply by writing to you, but the free books and gift will be mine to keep in any case.
I am over 18 years of age.

NO STAMP NEEDED

1EP5D

Ms/Mrs/Miss/Mr _____

Address _____

_____

_____ Postcode _____

Offer closes 30th June 1995. The right is reserved to refuse an application and change the terms of this offer. *Prices subject to change without notice. One application per household. Offer not available for current subscribers to this series. Valid in U.K. and Eire only. Overseas readers please write for details. Southern Africa write to: IBS Private Bag X3010, Randburg 2125.

MPS MAILING PREFERENCE SERVICE

You may be mailed with offers from other reputable companies as a result of this application. Please tick box if you would prefer not to receive such offers. ☐